The Battle
for
Harenburg Hill

ELIZABETH CALDER

D.O.L.L.

WOMEN

book series

D.O.L.L.

Daughters of Love & Light
www.daughtersofloveandlight.com
Adelaide, South Australia
admin@daughtersofloveandlight.com

ISBN: 9780645095128

All Scripture quotations, unless otherwise indicated, are taken from the Holy Bible, New International Version®, NIV®. Copyright ©1973, 1978, 1984, 2011 by Biblica, Inc.™

Publisher's Note: This novel is a work of fiction. Names, characters, places, and incidents are either products of the author's imagination or used fictitiously. All characters are fictional, and any similarity to people living or dead is purely coincidental.

Hymn lyrics in public domain: *Trust & Obey*, John H. Sammis 1887; *What a friend we have in Jesus*, Joseph M. Scriven, 1855.

Cataloguing-in-Publications entry is available from the National Library of Australia
http:/catalogue.nla.gov.au

Second edition published 2021

Dedication

for my beloved husband —
my silent partner in this adventure.

'Such confidence we have through Christ before God. Not that we are competent in ourselves to claim anything for ourselves, but our competence comes from God.'

2 Corinthians 3:4-5

Chapter 1

Ablue morning dawned as Wren's new reality loomed on the horizon. Outside the haze of cough syrup and pseudoephedrine, the fifty-kilometre span of flaxen grass fields somehow lost all romance. On the other side of her two-hour drive, the small township of Brite waited, unassuming as a speck of dust on the edge of the world. And yet as the sun rose warming her surroundings with its golden touch, the white steeple of the old church caught the light. It was the same light that now danced across Wren's hands as she loosened her grip on the steering wheel and peered up at the quaint house of worship.

Harenburg Hill.

It wasn't nearly as intimidating as its title. Though Wren couldn't help but sense it staring back at her, trying to be imposing from its grand hilltop.

Wren crawled the car up Main Street – the only street really – and was surprised to see the townspeople about so early on a Saturday morning. Without fail, each of them peered through the windshield at her as though she were an exotic animal in captivity. She subtly urged the accelerator before turning up the dirt road leading to Harenburg Hill.

Her eyes felt the weight of her lingering cold combined with the four a.m. wake up. Donning her black sunglasses and the three-inch heels she'd left strewn on the passenger seat, Wren stumbled out of the car, determined to look every part the short-awaited Reverend Wren Finley. All she lacked was a dog-collar.

'Good morning,' a pristine lady beckoned from the sage double-doors. Anyone would think it was Sunday with her mother-of-the-bride navy suit, opaque pantyhose, and kitten heels. At six a.m. in the morning, no less. Not to mention her perfectly coiffed perm.

Wren swiftly ran her fingers through her own strawberry-blonde waves, hoping none of them would snag a knot. Then she reached out her hand. 'Morning! I'm—'

'Oh, I know *exactly* who you are,' the lady replied, taking both of Wren's hands into her own and nursing them fondly. 'You must be *Mrs* Finley. I'm Mrs Margery Jones, the secretary here at Harenburg Hill.' Margery peered over Wren's shoulder. 'And, pray tell, where is the reverend?'

Pray tell? Wren swallowed the lump rising in her throat and opened her mouth to remedy the situation.

'Or did you come up early?' Margery went on. 'Perhaps to tend to the Manse? Add a few homely touches before your husband arrives?'

Once more, Wren opened her mouth to speak but found herself curiously distracted by the odd way in which Margery Jones fondled her left hand. She watched Margery's expression of fondness melt as she found Wren's ring finger ashamedly empty.

'There must have been a miscommunication,' Wren said at last. '*I'm* Reverend Finley. But please, just call me Wren.

Or *Pastor* Wren, if you prefer. Doesn't sound quite as formal, does it?'

Margery Jones dropped her hands at once. She stood cold and stiff, her mouth flattening into a cool line of steel. Her eyes seemed the only part of her that remained alive, burning with what Wren could only translate as contempt.

'You must be tired,' she said solemnly, not forgetting her country manners. 'The Manse is a little way down the lane. No doubt the elders will summon you momentarily.'

❧

Three Days Earlier

'We're almost there.' Liam grinned at her from the driver's seat.

Wren rolled her eyes. 'Since when are *you* romantic?'

His dark brow creased for a moment before he set his gaze back on the wide stretch of road before them. 'Let's just say it's a special occasion.'

'It's Wednesday.'

'What, and you don't think God works miracles on Wednesdays?'

Wren shrugged. 'To be honest, I don't think I've truly witnessed many miracles in my life so I'm not the greatest judge.'

'You found me,' he said with a wry grin. 'And you passed your masters with honours. I'd say that's a miracle…'

'As I remember it, *you* hunted me down and demanded I date you.'

'I don't recall being that forceful,' he said. 'I believe my exact words were – I had a dream about you last night and I believe you're the woman God wants me to marry.'

'Yeah, gee, no pressure.' She giggled. 'How's that going for you anyway? Four and a half years later?'

Liam shifted uneasily in his seat, pretending to look up at the sky. 'It looks like rain, I reckon.'

'Pfft, we're in the middle of summer. It's unlikely.'

Half-an-hour later, Wren and Liam sat in the carpark of a picturesque reserve surrounded by grey clouds and pelting rain. The wicker basket sat on the dashboard as they drank sparkling wine from plastic cups and nibbled on cheese, crackers, and dips.

'I can't believe this,' Liam muttered as he reached for a sandwich.

Wren went to find hers but stumbled across a small red velvet box. She glanced over at Liam, who was still studying the weather outside his window, and for reasons unbeknownst to her, she took the ring box and slipped it into her handbag. She then quietly sat back and peeled the layers of cling-wrap from her sandwich.

Her heart thudded in her chest, rising to her ears. It was all she could hear. All consuming thumping of absolute fear. But she wanted this – didn't she? It was all part of her five-year plan. Liam already had a house and a reliable family car. She had moved back with her foster mum to save money. They had both completed their theological degrees and landed associate pastoral positions in the same church. Everyone called them the dream team. Liam had even stepped down from leading worship so he could concentrate on his new ministry.

'Living Hope offered me the senior pastoral position,' he said with a sigh.

'What?' Wren's heartbeat began to steady with the injection of genuine godly pride. 'That's amazing. Congratulations!'

'Yeah, I had hoped to tell you in this beautiful spot I found. It was meant to be better than this…'

'Hey, it's okay,' she said, taking hold of his hand. She offered a small smile and a squeeze, glancing down at their contrasting skin tones — hers as white as an Englishman who never saw the sun, and his as dark as a short glass of bourbon. Being different was what they had always had in common. Two foster kids from the wrong side of everywhere somehow coming to know Christ. It was the storybook ending for any inspirational testimony.

'In that case.' He cleared his throat and reached for the basket. 'There's something—'

She instantly drew away from him — as far as she could in the front seat of a sedan — and dropped his hand. 'Please don't.'

Deep onyx eyes burned into her as though trying to conjure her meaning. 'What?'

'Please don't ask me,' she whispered.

He slowly reclined and stared out the windshield.

'I'm sorry.' She tugged the red velvet box from her bag and placed it in the cup holder between them. 'I just can't.'

Liam smoothed his hand over his after-five stubble. 'Do you need more time?'

'I don't know, I just saw it in there, and I freaked and I just… I'm so sorry. This shouldn't be my reaction. I don't know where it's coming from.'

'I don't get it.'

Wren glanced over at him to see his eyes rolled up toward the roof of the car. She knew he wasn't talking to her anymore. 'I'm sorry,' she whispered again.

Without another word, Liam calmly started the car. He packed up what was left of the picnic and lowered the basket into the backseat.

Then rather obscurely, Wren sneezed.

'Bless you,' he said gently, then looked over at her. 'Are you cold?'

'It must just be the change of weather or the pollen or something.'

He nodded slowly. 'In any case, let's get you home.'

Chapter 2

The following morning while it was still dark, Wren woke with a heavy head and an even heavier heart. Scooping her Bible and journal from the nightstand, she followed the familiar hallway of her childhood home to the small kitchen at the back. She tapped the floor lamp as she circled the dining table, laying the books down, before filling and boiling the kettle. With a cup of instant coffee in hand, she curled herself up in a dining chair and opened her Bible.

Right. You're going to have to explain this to me.

She peered over the random page searching for something – anything – some answer for the prodding she had received yesterday. Where had that fear come from? Had she truly listened to the Holy Spirit or was it her own insecurities rearing their ugly heads? The ones that told her, 'Everyone leaves, so don't get attached'… 'No one actually loves you'… 'Oh you think you can forget the past? Don't you remember what you've done…?'

She shook the words off and cracked open her journal. Taking the pen from the spiral binding, she began to jot down any verses that seemed the least bit interesting. Though none of them seemed to mention rejecting a perfectly nice Christian man when he proposes…

'I commend to you our sister Phoebe,' Wren whispered, following the black and white text of Romans 16 with her finger, *'a deacon of the church in Cenchreae.'* She cleared the tickle in her throat. *'I ask you to receive her in the Lord in a way worthy of his people and to give her any help she may need from you, for she has been the benefactor of many people, including me…'* Wren snagged a tissue from the box nearby and wiped her leaking nose. *'Greet Priscilla and Aquila, my co-workers in Christ Jesus. They risked their lives for me. Not only I but all the churches of the Gentiles are grateful to them…'* An almighty sneeze snuck up on Wren, before she could reach another tissue.

She glanced down at the splatters on the thin page. 'Hmm… sorry, Lord…'

'Aren't you well?' Mum wandered into the kitchen, kissing Wren's hair before reboiling the kettle.

'Do you think I made a mistake?' Wren asked at last.

Mum spooned coffee into her mug. 'What does Jesus have to say about it?'

'Not much.' She glanced down at her empty ring finger. She could have been engaged today. She could have been on her way to having everything she ever wanted. A real family. Someone who truly wanted her.

'Well, I don't know,' Mum said. 'I did think it a bit strange you two courting for so long. I mean, they say when you know you know.'

'And if you don't know?'

Mum gave her a stern look which broke into a smile. 'Then you don't marry them.'

Wren nodded slowly, reaching for another tissue.

Mum pressed the back of her hand to Wren's forehead. 'Baby, you're burning up.

Maybe you should go back to bed and I'll bring you some breakfast.'

Sniffling, Wren took her Bible and journal back to the bedroom with the addition of her laptop. Sprawling them out on the bed, she was determined to get to the bottom of this. Perhaps Mum had a point, she and Liam had been together so long, but something was missing. The butterflies? The romance? The knowing? All of the above?

But Liam was her best friend. Surely that counted for something.

She checked her phone. No 'good morning' text. And she knew he was awake. He was always awake before dawn, studying God's Word and spending quality time in prayer. Just like a man of faith ought to be. He was as perfect as they came. Sure, he had a past, who didn't? It was covered by grace now and God was certainly doing a good work in him. Liam's testimony was heartbreaking, he didn't receive what Wren did growing up – the steadiness of a good Christian foster family. Even though she didn't appreciate it at the time, she knew that was when God was beginning a good work in her too, she had just been too young and scared to see it. Now, on the other side of thirty, she could appreciate it for what it was – God's incredible grace over her life.

Please tell me what to do, she prayed in her heart. *I don't even feel like I can go back to Living Hope after this. Please...*

She opened her laptop, prepared to write an email to that effect to the elders, explaining she needed some time off. That was when she saw it. An unassuming email from Esther, Liam's sister. Obviously, he hadn't told her what happened...

> Check out this adorable church!
> It came up on job listings – way
> too far away of course, lol. But
> how cute is it!

Wren clicked to view the job listing to find an old Presbyterian church complete with a steeple and bell, its ornate sage green double-doors open in anticipation of the temporary minister. It looked like something out of a dream – Harenburg Hill of the township of Brite.

Wren only had one question. Where on earth was Brite?

She looked to the window as the first golden light began to stream through the curtains. *Really?* She sniffled then sighed. What did she have to lose? *Well, if I apply and I'm not meant to do it, don't even let me get a response.*

As the sun filled day dragged on with Wren in bed, her head grew heavier, her sinuses ached, and a seemingly harmless cough made her voice hoarse.

'Where did this even come from?' Mum asked, handing her a cup of lemon, ginger, and honey tea.

'Esther, actually,' Wren croaked.

'Was she sick on Sunday?'

'Sorry? What, no. I mean, I have no idea.' She tried to catch up with Mum's train of thought, despite her own fogginess. 'But you must admit, I do sound like a man. Who'll want to marry me now…'

Mum laughed. 'The man God hand-picked for you. In sickness and in health, remember?'

'You know that's not actually in the Bible, yeah?' Wren shook her head wearily and wiped her burning-red nose with a tissue. 'I should've accepted Liam while I had the chance. Do you have any idea how good his chicken noodle soup is?' She prostrated on the bed, shielding her eyes with the sleeve of her pyjamas.

'Better than mine?'

Wren shifted her arm and nodded.

'Well, I'll have to ask him for the recipe.'

She shot upright. 'Don't you dare!'

Then Wren's smart phone began to vibrate.

'I'll let you get that,' Mum said with a knowing smile.

Eagerly, Wren reached for the phone, expecting to see Liam's profile photo gaze lovingly back at her. But it wasn't him. It was a landline number. Who even had landline numbers anymore?

'Hello,' she rasped before attempting to clear her throat. 'Hello, Wren Finley.'

'Good morning, this is Trevor Burns from Harenburg Hill,' he said with a kind calm voice. 'I'm calling in regard to your job application…'

Chapter 3

Three days earlier, Wren thought she felt the confirmation of the Holy Spirit in her complete lack of uncertainty.

'I'll take it,' she found herself saying before doubt could creep in.

It astonished her that she could refuse a good man whom she had known for over ten years and loved for the better part of them, and yet when a church in the middle of nowhere said its elderly worn out reverend required a stress-induced operation but had been avoiding it due to his own stubbornness and inability to find someone willing to fill the role even after a six month search, she accepted the offer without hesitation. Was it the desperation in Trevor Burns' voice that ignited her need to be needed?

Or was it that God was actually opening a door? Albeit a temporary rotating door that could spit her back out once the reverend recovered.

She had prayed over the contract – the one they had finally managed to email after several failed attempts – and she had felt a pull she hadn't felt since she decided to go to Bible college. Five years later, with a Masters' degree and an associate pastoral role at Living Hope already under her belt, she felt ready for this. Dare she even say *called*. It was an urge far beyond the physical, unlike her relentless coughing, sneezing, and blowing of her nose. It was a spiritual urge. God was trying to tell her something. Or at least, that's what she had thought. Until she met Margery Jones.

When Wren was finally safe inside the farmhouse Margery had proudly referred to as 'The Manse', she kicked off her heels and dropped her bags on the hardwood floors before sinking to her knees. With the front door still wide open behind her, she bowed her heavy head.

'Please Lord… please tell me it was You who brought me here and not me? I thought I could do this but I'm completely incapable. You knew they were expecting a man. I know there's the contract but… but surely, they can just kick me out, right? What will I tell everyone at Living Hope? Mum? *Liam*? Urgh, Liam… he's going to think…' She shook her head. 'Please, Lord, just look after him. And comfort him. Please, Lord…'

Wren pulled her phone out from inside her blazer. No missed calls. No reception. Though something inside the farmhouse was ringing…

It was the faint *bring* of an old landline chiming from the next room. Climbing to her feet, she followed the sound to a peppermint painted kitchen with a retro Kelvinator, a rusted oven, and a ceramic sink the size in which one could bath a Great Dane. The phone hung on a nearby wall, its coiled line knotted. She leaned against the doorframe as she picked up the receiver, if only so it wouldn't bounce back out of her hand.

'Hello, Wren Finley?'

'Good morning *Ms* Finley, it's Trevor Burns.'

She ignored the way he emphasised her title. 'Hello, Mr Burns. Lovely to speak to you again.'

'Yes… about that… you sounded different the other day…'

Yes, she sounded like a man. 'I believe I explained at the time I was unwell with a cold?' Mutters muffled the line. She went on. 'Am I on speaker, Mr Burns?'

'Ms Finley,' another voice began, this one sterner. 'Neil Sutherland.'

Wren smirked. 'Hi Neil, what can I do for you?'

More muttering.

'I have advised the elders of the miscommunication,' Margery Jones' icy voice pierced Wren's ears. Was the whole congregation involved in their conversation?

'Now,' Margery continued, 'the elders are willing to re-negotiate the contract…'

'Ahem, thank you, Margery,' Neil said, seemingly recovering himself. 'What Mrs Jones means to say is that we, as an eldership, can relieve you of your pastoral duties since they may be…' He cleared his throat again. 'Well, if you feel, that in hindsight…'

'Yes?' she prodded. There was silence for a long moment, so Wren took it as her opportunity to speak. 'Don't worry. I've already prepared the sermon for tomorrow along the similar lines as to the three I supplied with my CV. I assume there weren't any theological discrepancies the eldership felt needed to be addressed beforehand?' Wren knew they were probably all thinking the fact that a woman shouldn't be preaching at all! But then, there was a little thing called discrimination…

'Very good… *Reverend*,' another male voice, far meeker than the others, offered before politely concluding the phone call.

The receiver tumbled from Wren's hands and she drifted back to the living room where her bags, shoes and life were all strewn haphazardly. She locked the front door – something she expected they didn't do in Brite as the lock itself was quite stiff – before retrieving her Bible, journal, and laptop. Clutching them to her chest, she wandered from one room to the other.

Lord, help me. Help me in this place…

By the time she reached the master bedroom with its ornate white iron bed, she collapsed. Sprawling out, she opened her copy of God's Word, praying all the while. That was when she realised her hands were shaking as she nervously tore through the scritta paper pages. Somehow, she landed in 2 Corinthians, her eyes catching on the scholar-given paragraph title: "Ministers of the New Covenant". She read on, eager to find a slice of encouragement. Tears pricked her over-tired and slightly irritated eyes. She blinked, once again splotching the page with ill-timed bodily fluids.

Such confidence we have through Christ before God,' she read aloud from chapter three, verse four, *'Not that we are competent in ourselves to claim anything for ourselves, but our competence comes from God.'* She sighed. 'May God bless the reading of His Word…'

Chapter 4

Insomnia struck in the early hours of Sunday morning and Wren knew she needed more than mere caffeine to get through this day. In this unfamiliar place, Wren began with the bedside lamp followed by the hallway light. She then switched on the external sconces and, with the comfort of God's Word in her hands, she curled up on the porch swing. It was too early even for Brite to be awake. In the middle of nowhere, she breathed deep and gazed up at the immense constellation of stars overhead. There were no streetlamps to interfere with the beauty. Darkness lingered over the township of Brite and yet Harenburg Hill still managed to reflect the moonlight like a beacon of hope on the hilltop. She opened her Bible to 2 Corinthians once more and set it down on the cushion beside her. Then she prayed. Her heart, mind, body and soul pressed into every word as she committed the congregation of Harenburg Hill to the Lord. She prayed for Margery Jones and Neil Sutherland by name. For Trevor Burns and for the owner of that meek voice who had offered her the only ounce of recognition. She prayed that the people of Harenburg Hill would be *'a letter from Christ... written not with ink but with the Spirit of the living God, not on tablets of stone but on tablets of human hearts...'* Just as Paul had written to the church at Corinth, so she prayed for this congregation. She prayed that her presence – as a woman – would not cause others to stumble. After all, God brought her here for a reason. Even if that reason would be short-lived.

After a morning of prayer and fasting, Wren washed and dressed and began to feel a little more like herself. Her cold was clearing – as was the fog of confusion from yesterday – and her heels were high enough to counteract her petite stature. Still, when she found the ceremonial robe and sash in the wardrobe, her slight shoulders drowned in them.

Wren arrived at Harenburg Hill by eight a.m. ready for her first task of the day – Sunday School. To her surprise, she was the first to arrive. Tentatively, she stepped inside, peering this way and that, taking in the rich carpets, the corbelled pews, and the gild-framed paintings of Bible stories. Her eyes lingered on one of Jesus on a white horse, gleaming, surrounded by heavenly beings and wielding a great sword. She smiled to herself. *He* was the one who brought her here. And *He* didn't make mistakes.

She slipped into the front pew, placing her Bible down beside her along with her sermon notes. 'Lord, bless this house of worship,' she whispered. 'Bless Harenburg Hill.'

'He already has,' Margery Jones said curtly from behind her.

Wren tried to hide her surprise. 'Good morning, Mrs Jones.'

A prim Margery Jones in her Sunday best strode straight past to the Hymn board and began to adjust the numbers. 'I see you've made yourself at home.'

'I thought I might have seen some of the children by now?'

Margery glared over her shoulder. '*Children?* Why would there be *children* here at this time of the morning?'

Wren restrained her carnal urge for sarcasm. 'For Sunday School? According to the contract—'

'Oh, that.' Margery focused her attention on the Hymn board again. 'That is only if we have children in the congregation, which we do not.'

Wren thought of the countless children at Living Hope in the over-crowded Sunday school classrooms. 'None?'

'Don't sound so shocked. Harenburg Hill is a *traditional* house of worship. It is not to everyone's tastes.'

'So, there's another church in Brite?' Wren asked.

'No. There are *other* churches in the surrounding towns. If the townspeople are serious about their faith and don't wish to worship at Harenburg Hill, then they will make the investment in their own spiritual lives and travel there.'

Wren simply nodded. 'In that case, where is my office?'

Once again, Margery's eyes betrayed her horror, but her mannerisms remained respectful as she delicately pointed the way. 'The reverend's office is down that hall, second door on the left.'

'Thank you.' Wren promptly followed the directions, if only to keep Margery Jones from glaring at her.

Wren found the office dark, stale, and musty, but otherwise quaint. A whole wall was dedicated to shelves of commentaries and other theological books. The large mahogany desk was emptied of the previous reverend's personal belongings and was simply adorned with a novelty quill and ink pot set and a study lamp. She placed her own belongings beside them before opening the blinds. The windows, however, were severely stuck and wouldn't budge – she supposed she'd have to have one of the handymen in town look at them. Old Testament and New Testament maps were framed and hung on the wall beside her and below them was a stout bookcase with only a single jar of random stationery. No doubt it was another place for the reverend's personal references. If she was here long enough, she might even ask Mum to send some of her textbooks to fill it.

As she settled into the office, reading through her notes and having yet another time of prayer, she suddenly heard the almighty shrill of the organ. She glanced at her watch. It must have been the music to greet the congregation. Unfortunately, Wren had heard more joyful music at funerals. Still, she stood up straight, pushed her shoulders back, and reached for her Bible and notes. With a deep breath and a slow exhale, she marched in her three-inch heels toward the door, praying in her heart all the while. She reached to turn the doorknob. She then began to rattle it. In one last attempt, she yanked at it, forcing herself to stumble backward. It was only then that she discovered the haunting truth – someone had locked her inside.

Fury burned hot beneath her skin and her heart thumped wildly within her. Her fingers dug into her Bible and she gritted her teeth. 'Not today,' she muttered, glancing back at the seemingly fused windows. Her glare was then caught by that very jar of random stationery, which rather divinely included a Stanley knife and a metal ruler. 'In Jesus name,' she muttered, '*not* today!'

Chapter 5

'Trust and obey. For there's no o-ther way. To be happy in Je-sus. But to trust and obey.'

Such triumphant words were seldom sung so solemnly. As Wren lingered in the entrance way, watching the two-dozen congregants with their heads either deep in the scarlet book or glancing around at the paintings, her heart ached.

In the same front pew of which Wren had mistakenly "made herself at home", stood Margery Jones alongside four older gentlemen. The most rotund of them – as tall as he was wide – stood next to a languid fair woman, a good ten years his junior. Beside her, sat a shady looking younger man in a long-sleeved shirt and jeans. Even from a distance, Wren could see his tattooed sleeves peeking out from each white cuff.

Then in fellowship sweet... we will sit at His feet... Or we'll walk by His side in the way...'

After a deep breath, Wren stepped forward to proceed down the aisle and lifted her own voice in song. She may not have had Liam's musical talent, but she knew her voice could be good, strong and loud. So, without a second thought, she belted it out. *What He says we will do; Where He sends, we will go...'*

Margery Jones dropped her hymnal.

'Never fear, only trust and obey...'

The voices of the congregation dwindled and soon it was only a few strays, the almighty organ, and Wren. *Trust and obey. For there's no o-ther way. To be happy in Je-sus. But to trust and obey.'*

Wren nodded to Margery as she strode to the pulpit. When the organist spied her, the hymn came to a discordant halt from which there was no coming back. Wren cleared her throat and laid her Bible and notes down.

Please Jesus, help me.

She offered a smile to the congregation before inviting them to be seated. The front row took their time in this, though Wren was encouraged when she saw a blonde woman smirk from the second row, before her equally fair husband flashed a genuine smile.

'Apologies for my late arrival,' Wren began. 'I'm Reverend Finley.' She paused to allow for the expected whispers. 'The eldership was kind enough to offer me the position while Reverend George Williamson is recovering from surgery.' At least her time in the office had allowed her to do some research on the shoes she was attempting to fill. She even found some of his old sermons in the filing cabinet. 'If you would all like to turn in your Bibles to Ephesians chapter one, then we'll open with a word of prayer…'

Wren cracked her own Bible open then glanced up. Not a single person had followed her instruction. Namely because, not a single person had a Bible on their person. She stood dumbfounded for a long moment before attempting to recover herself. She cleared her throat and leaned into the microphone. 'For those who don't have a personal copy of God's Word with them, I believe there are some available in the entrance way beside the hymnals. Some people may just have to share.'

Then she waited.

The blonde in the second row was the first one out of her seat. Wren and half the congregation watched in awkward silence as she made her way down the length of the aisle and back again, before opening the Bible and setting it between her and her husband.

'Whenever you're ready,' Wren said, stepping away from the pulpit.

Margery Jones and co shifted in the front row, occasionally looking at each other. Slowly, however, the rest of the congregation stood up and retrieved a Bible from the entrance way, and the church was suddenly filled with the sound of turning pages.

'And don't be afraid to use the concordance in the front if you need to,' Wren said, holding up her own weathered copy of God's Word. 'That's what it's there for. It's on page seven-hundred-and-seventy-nine in mine.'

Some in the congregation glanced up.

She grinned. 'But that's not going to help you very much.'

A genuine giggle arose in some places of the church, but the front row remained frozen, all except for the young man on the end, who didn't seem like he wanted to be there at all.

'Well, that's most of us now, I think,' Wren said, glancing at the front row. 'Let's commit our reading and this service to the Lord this morning…'

As the service came to a close, Wren habitually stood at the exit, expecting to meet the members of the congregation. However, one by one, they shuffled past her without so much as a 'hello'. Some mumbled, others offered a brief nod. Most scarcely made eye contact as though femininity was a severely contagious and cureless disease.

Then the blonde woman from the second row emerged, holding up the modest traffic of congregants, much to their frustration. With a warm smile, she shook Wren's hand. 'Beautiful sermon, Reverend,' she said. 'It was so encouraging. I'm Clare Sutherland and this is my husband Sean.'

'It's a pleasure to finally meet you, Reverend,' Sean said with a grin. 'I hear you've caused quite a revolution around here already.'

Their warm manner released the tension in Wren's shoulders. 'Believe me, it was unintentional. And please, call me Wren.'

'It's so nice to meet you,' Clare said, touching her arm.

However, the token of friendship briefly shifted Clare's chiffon blouse, and, from the corner of her eye, Wren saw fresh violet fingerprints and a smear of red upon the exposed arm. She swiftly averted her attention, conscious to keep her smile intact.

As Clare and Sean moved on, seemingly unaware that Wren had noticed anything, the young man stomped past her without so much as a glance. Then, the remainder of the front row trailed out onto the yellowing lawn.

'Neil Sutherland,' the corpulent man announced. 'And this is my wife, Judith.'

No hands were offered, so Wren kept hers to herself. 'I believe I just met a couple of your relations?'

'Our eldest son Sean and his wife Clare,' Judith replied in a quiet yet matter-of-fact tone. 'And our youngest son, Frank, was seated with us.'

'This is Trevor Burns,' Margery said, gesturing to a true-blue leathery skinned man. 'And this is Donald and Peter.'

The hierarchy was inescapable. It was clear in the reverend's absence, Neil was the intimidating regent of Harenburg Hill, while Margery was the matriarch over the administration side. Trevor had kind eyes in a hard face and seemed to get stuck with the dirty work. Donald looked every bit the old grandfather, past his preaching prime, but content to be somewhat involved. And then there was Peter. On closer approach, Peter was slightly hunch-backed yet willowy in stature. He had a hooked nose on which a pair of thick glasses rested, patched up with electrical tape in the middle. The moment he held out his hand to her, she knew he was the meek voice she had heard on the phone.

Wren shook his hand and smiled. 'It's a pleasure to meet you.'

'Well, it has been a trialling day for us all, I'm sure,' Margery said with a stiff smile, and began her careful descent down the hill.

'Enjoy the rest of your Sunday,' Wren replied. 'I'll be in my office if anyone needs me.'

They all paused.

Donald peered back at her. 'On a Sunday?'

'Of course,' Wren replied. 'I like to spend some quiet time with the Lord in His house after the service. There's nothing quite like it.'

Neil grunted before leading the way from Harenburg Hill.

Chapter 6

By Monday morning, the township of Brite was well aware of their most recent arrival notching their population up to a total of three-hundred-and-thirty-six as opposed to the neat three-hundred-and-thirty-five to which they had grown accustomed.

By Tuesday morning, Wren was ready to face the town head on in a desperate search for caffeine. Kris' Café seemed the only promising prospect if she didn't want to settle for the single brand of instant from the general store.

'Welcome to—' the brunette behind the counter began before her face twisted into the widest of smiles. 'You must be Wren Finley!'

The bell over the door had scarcely stopped ringing before the woman folded Wren in her plaid-shirt covered arms.

'Hello,' Wren said breathlessly, slightly taken aback.

'I'm Kris.' She beamed. 'Come in, come in…'

Wren wanted to but she felt like she was stuck in a time warp. She had assumed from the outside that the café simply hadn't updated their window display since the holiday season. But this was not the case. In the far corner of the café stood a real six-foot Christmas tree in a pot, its forest scented foliage glistening with fairy lights and decorations of red, green, and gold. An antique train set circled the tree, guarding the fanciful presents piled beneath it. Over the unlit fireplace hung striped stockings, each with their own name – Bruce, Rosemary, Kris, Oliver, and Ava. Only Bruce's appeared to be full. Holly wound around support posts. Mistletoe hung over the door to the restrooms. And each intimate table setting was complete with baubles, a candle and a Christmas-themed menu. The furthest wall housed bookcases with wooden toys, scented candles, Christmas storybooks, and other gifts. Wren suddenly felt like she had walked into a Hallmark film in which happy endings weren't only possible, they were inevitable.

'I must say our eggnog is particularly good,' Kris said, 'but you look like you could do with a coffee.'

Wren glanced around. The place was empty of customers except for Trevor Burns who sat in the far corner by the tree reading the local paper. 'Yes, sorry, yes, that would be wonderful.'

Kris grinned as she churned the grinder to life. 'Rough week, hey? I hate to tell you, it's only Tuesday.'

'I'm well aware.' Wren smiled as she perched on a stool at the counter. 'I have to say, this place is absolutely magical.'

'Cheers,' Kris called over the heating milk. 'I grew up in a family who loved Christmas. It's in our blood.'

Wren looked past the coffee machine to the ornate nativity scene on the back bench over which hung an engraved metal sign: *For unto us a child is born, to us a son is given, and the government will be on his shoulders. And he will be called Wonderful Counsellor, Mighty God, Everlasting Father, Prince of Peace.'* Wren pointed. 'Hey, that's from the book of Isaiah.'

'Yeah, beautiful, isn't it? Bruce made that,' Kris said, placing the coffee on the counter.

'Is that why he has so many gifts in his stocking?' Wren asked before taking her first sip. She absentmindedly sighed. She then held the mug with both hands, her petite frame melting around it.

'See, that's the reaction you want from a customer.' Kris smiled and sipped her own espresso. 'And no, Bruce is no longer with us, but I didn't have the heart to take the stocking down.'

'I'm so sorry,' Wren said, regaining her composure and forcing herself to put the coffee back on the counter. 'I have all day if you want to talk about it?'

'Nah, I'm okay. After Mum and Dad's divorce, Bruce was there for our family, but nothing really eventuated between him and

Mum. Sad for her, really. I think if they had more time, he would've made a pretty sweet stepdad.'

'I lost my foster dad when I was sixteen,' Wren said with a shrug. 'At least you didn't go off the rails like me.'

'Off the rails? *You*?'

Wren's eyes widened as she nodded. 'I almost ended up in juvie. Looking back, it was only prayer that kept me out. Mum's a pretty fierce prayer warrior.' Wren wasn't sure if Kris seemed impressed or amused. Either way, she meant it in a way to connect with her but before they could go any deeper, the doorbell chimed.

Kris glanced up. 'Speaking of legendary mums.'

Wren looked up to see an older lady with cropped auburn hair and a bright red-lipped smile. The young woman who followed her couldn't have been more opposite with her bohemian blonde waves, bare face, and round protruding belly from her otherwise thin frame.

'Wren,' Kris began, 'my mum Rosemary and my daughter Ava. I know what you're thinking, but she looks just like her dad. Believe me, she is mine. I still have the stretchmarks to prove it...'

Wren chuckled.

'Oh, Reverend, how lovely to meet you,' Rosemary said with a genuine smile that momentarily belonged to Wren then shifted. Wren followed it to the corner of the café where Trevor sat, a slight smirk on his face.

'Good morning Mr Burns!' Rosemary called with a wave.

He didn't look up, but Wren could see his smile widen. He lifted one hand. 'Rosemary!'

Ava stood rubbing her belly. 'Mum, are there any ginger snaps left?'

'Third jar.' Kris winked.

'Looks like you'll need another stocking soon,' Wren said.

'Yeah... it's been hard for her, you know. But she's made the best of it.' Kris lowered her voice as she leant on the counter. 'She said it was some guy passing through, spiked her drink or something. Anyway, maybe you could chat to her sometime.' Kris shrugged. 'It couldn't hurt, right?'

Wren's gaze softened and she reached out to squeeze Kris' hand. 'Of course, whenever she's ready.'

Kris drew back then and downed the remainder of her espresso. 'You must be wondering why none of us were at church on Sunday.'

'Honestly? Not really. I mean, I would love to see you there, but I understand it probably hasn't been… welcoming?'

'Ever since they found out about Ava.'

Wren nodded and sipped her coffee. 'I must say, either I have been completely deprived, or you make the best coffee I've ever tasted.'

'Bit of both.' Kris smirked. 'The first was on the house. Let me make you another.'

Chapter 7

Once she was sufficiently caffeinated, Wren stopped past the general store on her way up to Harenburg Hill. She supposed it was probably walking distance – only not in her shoes. As she entered her now unlocked office, she laid her purchases down on the desk: a new door knob set, a non-silicone solvent-free spray Google told her would work on hard to open windows, a jar of instant coffee for emergencies, some frozen meals, and a few blocks of chocolate – also for emergencies. She glanced from the old door handle to the new packeted one, figuring she could either spend the whole afternoon reading instructions or she could call the one person she knew would help her.

Glancing at her phone, it was the same old story – no missed calls and no reception. She scrolled through anyway and found Liam's number before using the landline in the hallway to call out. Within two rings, he was there.

'Hello, this is Liam.'

She paused for a moment, staring at the door handle.

'Hello?'

'Oh, hi… hey Liam, it's me.'

His tone instantly softened. 'Hey, you.'

Wren smiled.

'How's it all going in Woop Woop?'

'Good,' was her knee-jerk reaction, but then she remembered who she was speaking to. 'Actually, terrible. Somehow they thought I was a man and I got locked in my office so now I'm trying to change the door handle and I have no idea how to do it…'

'Right… I'm guessing it was a cold?'

'How did *you* know?'

'You always lose your voice when you're sick. And besides, your mum asked me for my chicken noodle soup recipe.'

Wren rolled her eyes. 'Of course, she did…'

'Apparently you said it was better than hers?'

'Well…'

He laughed down the phone. 'Right, well, anyway, getting back to the problem at hand. Do you have a small Phillips Head?'

'A what?'

'A screwdriver. The pointy kind.'

'Um, yeah, I think I saw a toolbox in the kitchen earlier… hold on a sec.' Wren left the phone dangling by the cord while she retrieved the tool. 'Okay,' she said, 'now what?'

He sighed. 'This is going to be a long one isn't it? Hang on, let me get comfortable…'

A couple of hours later with a brand-new doorknob only Wren had the keys to, she sat slumped on the hallway floor, the phone still pressed to her ear.

'I can't believe she actually locked you in there.' Liam chuckled.

'Believe me, it wasn't funny at the time.'

'Still, you handled yourself well. I would've been tempted to announce it in front of the congregation.'

'I can't take the credit,' she said honestly. 'It was all *Him*.'

'So, what are you preaching on this week?'

'Women's roles in the church.'

'Huh?'

Wren laughed. 'I'm kidding. I don't know, I'll probably just move on to Ephesians two, try to keep it nice and encouraging for them. For now…'

'So no fire and brimstone this week?'

'Not this week, no.' Wren grinned. She hadn't realised how much she missed him. And it was strange, as though something had changed between them for the better. Who knew rejecting a man's proposal could be so good for him? She shook her head. That wasn't fair. It wasn't like Liam was some sort of egocentric maniac. He was Liam. And right now, he felt like the Liam from seven years' ago, the one she used to crush on from afar before he told her about his dream, and it all seemed so serious.

'You still there?' he asked.

'Hmm? Yeah... but...'

'What is it?'

'Do you think I'm doing the right thing? By staying, I mean.'

'Wrenley,' he began, 'that's between you and God.'

She sighed, relishing in the way he used her pet name for the first time in forever. 'Well, I better go. Sermons don't write themselves.'

'I hear you. Senior pastor now, remember? I must admit I'm missing the music though.'

'Oh, yeah.' She buried her face in her palm. 'I'm so sorry, I didn't even ask...'

'Next time,' he said.

'Next time. Yes, definitely.'

She continued to grin long after the phone had been hung up. When she eventually peeled herself off the floor, she saw Clare marching down the hall followed by an apprehensive Judith. Wren snapped into pastoral mode, pushing her shoulders back and forcing her inappropriate smile into hiding. 'Clare? Judith? I wasn't expecting anyone today.'

'Can we come in?' Clare asked, holding her hand out to guide Judith's arm. 'It's important.'

'Of course, yes, sit down.' Wren stepped aside for them before making her way to the opposite side of the desk. She looked at Clare first. 'What seems to be the matter?'

Clare then turned to Judith who squirmed beside her. 'You have to tell her what you told me.'

Judith met Wren's eye. Was it shame or fear? Wren couldn't tell. Perhaps a bit of both?

'Mrs Sutherland,' Wren said gently. 'Anything you tell me will stay between us.'

'But it can't,' Judith snapped. 'You have to *do* something about it.'

Wren looked between the two women. 'I'm sorry?'

Clare's voice softened. 'The elders are planning a secret members' meeting to vote for you to be removed.'

Wren nodded and cleared her throat, trying to remain calm. She then reached for a block of chocolate and whacked it on the desk before unwrapping it and placing the foil and its broken pieces in the middle. 'I find this helps,' Wren said simply, popping a piece into her mouth.

Without hesitation, both Clare and Judith followed suit.

'So,' Wren began, manoeuvring the melting chocolate around in her mouth. 'When did you say this was happening?'

'Tonight, nine o'clock,' Judith replied from between chocolate-smeared teeth.

Wren was still nodding as she reached for another piece. 'When they know I won't be here.'

'We had to warn you,' Clare said.

Wren swallowed her fourth piece of chocolate before she could muster a reply. 'Why?'

Judith's mouth gaped open and her eyes bulged. 'What do you mean *why*? So you can stop them, of course!'

'Yes, but...' Wren swallowed the lump rising in her throat. 'I don't understand why you would go against your husband...' She then looked to Clare. 'Your father-in-law... who, you have to admit, is pretty darn scary. Why would you do that for me?'

Judith clasped Wren's hand and gave it a squeeze, leaving fingerprints of melted chocolate. 'Because it's about time someone stood up to them.'

'But what can I do? I'm not even technically a member.'

'Funny you mention that,' Judith said, her lips curling. 'Neither are they...'

Chapter 8

When the day was done, Wren left Harenburg Hill with her bag of frozen dinners. Then she waited until dark. At about eight-thirty p.m., she switched off all her lights and sat out on the porch, watching the hilltop. Only then were the church lights switched on. She watched cars slowly creep up the hill, headlights off. She watched the distant faces of two-dozen congregants pile into the building like ants into a nest, fearing being caught or stomped on.

Wren forsook her frozen dinner for a time of prayer and fasting, figuring the chocolate she ate earlier would give her the energy she required to climb that hill. So no one would be suspicious, she left her office door unlocked. In her lap, however, lay the only piece of evidence from inside needed for her defence. She pressed the book firmly to her chest and began her staggered march up the hill in a pair of leather boots she'd borrowed from Clare.

She knew it was still a risk. In fact, she was fairly certain she would be on her way home by dawn. But this book evened the playing field. She didn't like resolving to such tactics. In all of this, she knew she had to remain as innocent as a dove and as shrewd as a serpent. It was the only way this would work – with God, always.

She climbed through her well-lubricated office window and into the dark. Her stomach lurched within her. She could hear old Neil Sutherland's booming voice barrelling down the hallway toward her. Everything about this felt wrong. What kind of eldership summons their congregation at this time of night to undermine the minister they themselves hired? A single reference check would have straightened out their misconception. A face-to-face interview – if they had been patient enough to wait for one – would have certainly given them a clear indication as to who Wren Finley truly was. She couldn't help she had a unisex name. Her biological mother thought she was having a boy and even after Wren was born, her mother was convinced she was a boy. Doctors said it was the drugs that caused it all: the first stillbirth of Wren's elder half-brother; her mother's constant instability and neglect; and finally, her mother's inevitable overdose which sent Wren into the foster care system for good.

Wren blinked back the tears. Funny thing was, if the eldership of Harenburg Hill knew about her past, she doubted they would feel compassion on her. Instead they would probably find a faster way to be rid of her for fear that her broken life might be infectious.

She followed the light streaming into the dim hallway. Then, she stepped into it.

A collective gasp silenced Neil Sutherland and he followed their gaze to see Wren making her way toward the pulpit.

'Sorry, I seem to be late again,' she said. 'It seems I didn't get the memo.'

For a moment, everyone was silent, including Margery Jones who was set beside Neil on a hardwood chair, a clipboard in her hands.

Even from a distance, Wren could see there was only one item on the agenda.

'Ms Finley,' Neil began after a few moments, 'we are leaving the decision of your appointment to the members of the church, as our constitution states.'

Wren – now at least three heads shorter than him – nodded in agreement. 'I thought as much, so I brought the members' registry for your convenience.' The thick sage green book landed on the pulpit with a thump. 'Since I'm still the temporary reverend and I should take some responsibility, I took the liberty of checking the registry to see who exactly belonged in the church membership and who did not.'

Red splotches appeared on Neil's neck as he slowly opened the book.

'What does it say?' someone called from the congregation.

'Would you like to tell them, or should I?' Wren asked. 'According to your constitution, only the members are permitted to vote.' She lowered her voice. 'So, really, none of them should be here.'

Peter solemnly approached the pulpit, adjusting his glasses. 'If I may just have a look, we can have this matter sorted.'

Neil slunk back.

Margery Jones slowly lowered her clipboard to her lap and crossed her ankles.

Peering through his spectacles, Peter addressed the congregation with his usual gentility. 'It seems that many of our members are deceased. There are only two members officially registered.' He cleared his throat. 'One Reverend George Williamson, who of course is an apology this evening and…'

The air was thick with silent anticipation.

Peter slowly turned. 'And one Miss Margery Forsyth.'

Forsyth? Where had Wren heard that name before? She hadn't even imagined Margery Jones being anything but Margery Jones. But of course, she had to have a maiden name.

Wren's gaze travelled from Peter to Margery to Neil then stopped. The latter had lost his red spots and now appeared smug once more.

'It appears,' Peter said gently. 'There is only one *eligible* member.'

Margery Jones shifted uneasily in her chair as all eyes fell on her.

Wren glanced at Judith who uncharacteristically winked.

'As per the constitution, once this matter is voted on, it cannot be addressed again for a further twelve months.' Peter gently closed the book and cleared his throat once more. 'Margery Forsyth-Jones,' he said calmly, 'we are voting on the issue as to whether Reverend Wren Finley should remain in her appointed position. How do you vote? Yay or nay?' He paused then added. 'I obviously don't have to remind you of the impact your vote will have both on Reverend Finley and Harenburg Hill.'

After silent deliberation, Margery Jones looked straight at Wren. But there was no contempt in her eyes. No fire burning into her. No, if Wren wasn't mistaken, the look in Margery Jones' eyes was one of hope.

'Yay,' she whispered.

'You heard the woman!' Neil burst before registering the actual answer.

'Yes, I believe I did, but she may need to say it a little louder,' Peter said.

'Yay,' Margery Jones said with a brief roll of her eyes. 'I vote for Reverend Finley to remain in her appointed position.'

'What?!' Neil shouted.

Wren, however, couldn't speak. She wasn't sure whether to laugh or cry or just drop to her knees then and there and praise Jesus with her face to the floor.

'That settles it then,' Peter said, handing the members' registry to Wren. 'And I suggest you keep this somewhere safe.'

Chapter 9

As the church slowly emptied, Wren shared a knowing look with Clare and Judith before returning to her office. She locked both windows, returned the members' registry to the filing cabinet, then locked her office door behind her. She felt safe knowing only two keys existed – one on her key ring and the other in a peppermint-painted kitchen drawer at the farmhouse.

Completely overwhelmed by the happenings of the evening, Wren returned to the farmhouse exhaustedly content. She went to unlock her front door, ready for a good night's sleep. Only it wasn't locked. In fact, the door was slightly ajar. She peered inside. The only thing that seemed to be amiss was that the kitchen light had been left on. In all her anxiety, had she forgotten to turn it off? Surely, not. She swallowed the fear rising in her throat and made her way through the house, switching on all the lights. It couldn't have been a robbery. Everyone thought she was at home and her laptop was still on the dining room table. One by one she turned the lights off again before halting in the kitchen. There on the Kelvinator refrigerator beneath a faded magnet, hung a piece of paper. In the centre of the page, a single Bible verse was cut out and glued there: *'When he reached home, he took a knife and cut up his concubine, limb by limb, into twelve parts and sent them into all the areas of Israel.'*

Wren hurled the empty acidic contents of her stomach into the wide sink. Shaking, she took her car keys and her pile of work from the dining table and ran to the outside. Once inside the car, she locked the doors, panting.

'Please protect me, Lord…'

The engine roared to life and she spun the car around, heading straight for Harenburg Hill. Her mind raced. She didn't even know who to call or where to go? Where was the nearest police station? She had only seen the fire station in town.

Desperate for sanctuary, she raced into Harenburg Hill and ran into her office, locking the door behind her. She couldn't remember closing the front door or even turning off the car's ignition. All she knew was that she needed to be behind a locked door, safe from whoever left that verse in her kitchen. Her chest ached from her thumping heart and in one last brave effort, she unlocked her office door, grabbed the landline receiver, and hit the redial button.

'Wren?' Liam asked sleepily.

'I didn't know who else to call...'

'Woah.' His voice suddenly came to attention. 'What's wrong?'

'I had a threat... someone came into my house and... I had a threat. The verse... Judges... the... the...'

'Are you safe?' he asked desperately.

'I think so... I'm in the hallway but my office doesn't have a phone and...'

'What office doesn't have a phone!' he snapped. 'Does the cord reach? Under the door?'

Wren fumbled, dropping the receiver entirely before retrieving it once more and following the cord through under the crack of the door. She then locked herself in. 'Yes… okay…'

'Stay there and don't move, okay? No matter what. I may lose reception on my way, but I want you to stay right there, okay?'

'What are you talking about?' Wren cried. 'On your way *where*?!'

'I'm coming to you right now. I just closed the door behind me, okay? I'm on my way… just stay calm… let's pray together. We'll pray for two hours straight if we have to…'

As Liam began his prayer of protection through the Bluetooth speaker in his car, Wren sobbed against the office door and clutched the phone as hard as she could. Pangs of fear stabbed her insides. Her head felt light. There was a ringing, but it wasn't the phone. It was faraway. And the phone was still at her ear.

Deep breaths… Help me, Lord…

She listened to Liam's soothing voice until his phone lost reception. At least that meant he was close. Still, she clung to the landline receiver.

What would she do with her hands otherwise? They ached to wring something, to release the tension spreading from her neck to her shoulders and down her arms. Still, even her tight grasp couldn't stop her from trembling. There on the office floor, her body firm against the door, she could do nothing but pray in her heart. Her voice had given way at least an hour ago. For anytime she used it she spun into uncontrollable sobbing and heaving for breath.

Knotted. Every inch of her was knotted and twisted, holding the fear close within her chest. It was suffocating.

Then she heard a noise. She froze. Footsteps. Heavy urgent footsteps stomped down the hall. The sound reminded her of the way rebellious young Frank Sutherland stomped out of Harenburg Hill on Sunday. Surely, it couldn't be him. Time seemed to stand still for a moment until all she could hear was her heart thumping in her ears, consuming her body. Frank hadn't been at the meeting. He was the only one not at the meeting.

A gentle knock started Wren back into the moment.

'Wrenley, it's me,' Liam said softly through the door.

She knew why he used her pet name. Anyone else would think it inappropriate at such a time as this. But she knew, it was his way of letting her know she was safe.

She fumbled and staggered, unlocking the door with trembling hands before throwing herself into him. He felt solid and warm. His familiar smell of lemongrass soap lulled her as she buried her tear-smeared face into his chest. Strong arms wrapped around her, nursing her head as it rested against him.

'It's okay,' he hushed.

Wren lost track of all space and time as Liam continued to hold her. Her shaking faded into stillness. Her tears soaked into his shirt.

'I can't do this,' Wren whispered.

'Maybe not. But Jesus can…'

Chapter 10

Back at the farmhouse, Wren found the phone number for the police sergeant in the town over – it was scrawled messily in a small address book by the knotted phone. She pressed into the wall, her forehead against the doorframe. She understood a Bible verse wasn't exactly a direct threat, but someone had been in her home. Someone had put it on her fridge. Someone meant to frighten her enough to make her want to leave. And it was working. The sergeant assured her he would make an official report and recommended she change the locks as soon as possible – something Liam had already suggested.

'Everyone's talking about the new female minister in Brite,' the sergeant said. 'I just think you've ruffled a few people's feathers. It'll die down…'

His tactless choice of words sent a shiver down her spine. Still, he said he would collect the evidence at first light, in case there was anything to go by. At least that was a small comfort.

'You'll have to stay at the pub, I guess,' Wren said once she was off the phone, her thoughts leaping from one fear to another.

'I don't think you should be alone,' Liam replied.

'Well, I don't think it's very appropriate. I'm under fire enough as it is.'

He nodded slowly. 'Right. First thing tomorrow then. Once the sergeant comes, we'll check me into the pub.'

She sighed. It was one less thing for her to worry about. Even if she felt safer with Liam in the house.

'You should probably get some sleep,' he said, slumping into the couch beside her. 'I'll stay out here. Promise. No funny business.'

She glanced over at him, quickly enough to catch his wink. Something inside her fluttered. 'Thanks for the offer but I don't think I could sleep if I tried. I'd rather just sit here with all the lights on to be honest.'

'Fair call. Well, in that case, have you decided what to preach on this week yet?'

'Not yet,' she replied, not seeing the relevance to her predicament. 'Why's that?'

'Well, given the sergeant's comments, I reckon you might have a full house.'

Wren hadn't expected Liam's suspicions to be so well-founded. But to be sure, the townspeople's curiosity got the better of them and when the organist began her same pre-service funeral march, the pews were already full. Wren made a point to greet Kris, her husband Oliver, Rosemary and Ava, who kept glancing toward the front of the church.

'You know,' Wren began, taking the teen by the hand and snagging her brief attention. 'If you ever want to talk, my door is always open.'

Well, except for last Sunday morning, but we'll forget about that...

'Thanks.' She flashed a brief smile before leaning onto her toes and rubbing her belly as she continued to survey the front rows.

Kris looked curiously at her then back to Wren. 'Don't worry, she's probably just nervous being here after so long.'

'It's understandable,' Wren replied, but her own curiosity began to stir as to what Ava's connection was with the Sutherland family, since it was in their direction her attention seemed to linger. Perhaps it was them who exclusively forced her out of the church? Or perhaps there was more.

As Wren approached the front, she almost stumbled into Margery Jones who had just finished updating the hymn board.

'Good morning,' Wren said brightly. At least she could rule out Margery leaving that note in her house. After all, if she had wanted to get rid of her that badly, she had the perfect opportunity at the members' meeting. 'You know, about the other night…'

'I believe,' Margery began, 'we could have used the Sunday School this morning. There are quite a few young families here today.'

Wren exhaled. She wasn't going to make this easy. 'Yes, we do, don't we? It's very encouraging.'

'Mmm,' was Margery's reply. 'Speaking of visitors, do you happen to know that indigenous man over there?'

Wren's breath caught in her chest as she contemplated the tone of Margery's question. The way she sounded Liam's heritage as though he was a foreigner who needed to be returned to wherever he came from.

'Yes actually,' she said, mentally biting her tongue. 'That's the Senior Pastor from Living Hope Baptist Church in the city, Liam Smith. He came to visit and show some support while I settle in.'

Margery took in a sharp breath. 'Senior Pastor?'

'Mmm,' was all Wren replied before finding her seat beside him.

Wren had never felt more scrutinised than during that second service. The congregants not only brought their Bibles this week but notebooks and pens to take notes. Wren had considered tailoring a sermon in response to the threat she'd received, but she thought it better to ignore it. Instead, she remained in Ephesians and offered an encouraging word on the reconciliation between them and Christ. Whenever she said the word 'Gentile', young Frank Sutherland's face popped into her head and she had to mentally – and spiritually – push it away. She had no evidence to suspect him of anything.

After the service, Wren stood by the exit, her hand at the ready. Naturally, Kris hugged her, but the majority continued with their mumbles and dismissive waves as they left.

In amongst the cool greetings, however, Clare managed to break away from the Sutherlands and weave her way through to Wren before they could get there. 'Beautiful sermon, once again,' she said, her face aglow.

'Thank you so much,' Wren said, shaking the hand she offered.

Clare glanced back at the line of people behind her. Wren followed to see Sean pushing his way through. So before Clare could retract her hand, Wren gave it a squeeze.

'Should we meet at Kris' Café one day this week?' she said swiftly. 'You name the time.'

'Tuesday. Ten o'clock,' Clare replied, almost as if she had orchestrated the offer herself.

'Done,' Wren said in undertones before smiling broadly at Sean as he approached. 'Good morning!'

Sean breathed heavily but returned her warm greeting nonetheless before turning to his wife. 'You seemed to barrel out of there today,' he said with a chuckle.

'It was really stuffy,' Clare said. 'Didn't you think it was stuffy?' She took a deep breath. 'Ah, it's so much better out here. I thought I was going to faint.'

'Maybe you're pregnant after all,' Sean said with a wink.

'Well,' Clare stammered for a moment. 'Well, I guess if he can do it for Sarah. Who knows, eh?'

Sean wrapped his arm around his wife then tugged her forward. Had Wren not been as close in proximity, she wouldn't have seen the brief discomfort flash across Clare's face. She also wouldn't have seen the way he proceeded to take her by the arm – not the hand – to guide her down the hill.

Tuesday, ten a.m. She would have to wait until then.

Chapter 11

After what Margery Jones referred to as a week's grace, Wren's Monday morning began with a stack of manila files; a pile of unopened envelopes, attention 'The Reverend of Harenburg Hill'; and at least two-dozen membership forms which needed to be entered into the official registry – a task only the reverend of Harenburg Hill was entitled to do. It was almost enough to make Wren forget about the Bible verse that had hung on the Kelvinator. Almost.

'You wouldn't believe what I discovered today,' Wren said as she poured the jug of gravy over her schnitzel and chips. Dinner at the pub may not have been the healthiest option but it sure beat a frozen meal. 'Harenburg Hill needs to renew their subscription to Ministers'R'Us.'

'Sorry, *what?*' Liam coughed before washing his steak down with a cold beer. 'Do I even want to know what that is?'

'It's a sermon writing service,' Wren said simply. 'There was even a folder labelled "Winning sermons to recycle".'

'What did you do with it?'

'I recycled it.'

'How are we getting along here?' the bartender asked as she strutted over. She rested a hand on Liam's shoulder. 'Are we going to have another song later?'

Wren's eyes widened at him. 'Another song?'

He wiped his mouth with a napkin. 'Zoe, this is Wren.'

'The celebrity,' Zoe said. 'I've heard a lot about you.'

'It's nice to meet you, Zoe,' Wren said. 'Don't tell me you've got Liam singing for his supper?'

'Oh he loves it.' Zoe beamed and shook Liam by the shoulders. 'Don't ya.'

Wren watched Zoe float back to the bar where a group of tradies were waiting for their pints. 'Well, she seems nice.'

'What's that look for?' Liam asked.

'Nothing, I'm fine.'

'*Fine?*'

'Mmm,' Wren said and dug into her schnitzel.

'I only sang one song the other night,' Liam said. 'Her band cancelled last minute.'

'Really, I'm fine,' Wren said with a shrug. 'Anyway, after what happened the other week, it's not like I have any say.'

Liam's brow crumpled. 'You mean, any say over where I sing?'

'Or anything, I guess,' Wren said, forcing a smile. 'Anyway, thanks for dinner, but it's getting late.'

'You haven't finished your—'

'Good night,' she said, habitually leaning over to peck his cheek. Only there was nothing habitual about it. She paused, hovering near his cheek as the spark shocked her. Then she stepped back. But he leaned forward, half out of his chair.

'Stay,' he said, his eyes firm on hers.

Her mouth was dry. She shifted nervously beneath his intensity. 'I should really go,' she said in hushed tones. She watched his Adam's apple bounce in his throat followed by the brief pulse in his jaw. He clearly wanted to argue his point, but they were in foreign territory. They had gone from friendship to courtship so quickly, Wren couldn't remember a time she'd even flirted with Liam. It seemed their destinies had been decided for them and they had just gone along for the ride. Until now.

'Then call my room,' he said, 'when you get home. Let me know you're safe.'

'I will. I promise.'

And with that, she left. When she returned to the farmhouse, she followed through with her promise, only to hear the message bank for room three. Clearly, Liam had decided to stick around for a song as Zoe requested. Wren left a brief message, the phone almost bouncing out of her hand as she felt the urge to pace. She swiftly hung up before she made an even bigger fool of herself.

The following morning Wren went to Kris' Café as planned. Saving her caffeine fix for her meeting with Clare, she opted for a mug of eggnog.

'You won't regret this,' Kris said as she began to pour the boiling beverage.

Wren glanced around. Once again Trevor Burns sat in the far corner, only this time Rosemary was chatting happily to him.

'Here we go,' Kris said with a grin.

Wren took a deep drink then lowered the cup. 'Urgh, my goodness, that's incredible.'

'I know.' Kris poured herself a cup.

'Can I have some, too?' Ava asked as she adjusted her apron.

'Hmm, not sure if you're allowed, honey.'

Ava rolled her eyes. 'So many rules.'

Kris chuckled. 'So Reverend, what brings you to our humble place this morning?'

'I'm actually meeting Clare Sutherland,' Wren said brightly. 'She should be here any moment.'

Smash.

A frozen Ava peered down at the pieces of frosted glass and ginger snaps at her feet.

'What's the matter, hun?' her mother asked as she reached for the broom.

'Nothing,' Ava replied, shaking her head. 'Just baby brain, I guess.' The teen flustered and fumbled her way over the broken glass before tugging off her apron. 'I'll be at the back if anyone needs me.'

'Hormones, eh?' Kris muttered as she swept up the mess.

'Yeah, hormones.' Wren took another sip of eggnog and checked her watch.

'I wouldn't expect Clare to actually come,' Kris said casually.

'What do you mean?'

Kris shrugged. 'He may not look it, but that Sean is pretty controlling. Apple doesn't fall very far from the tree in that family.'

Wren was about to reply when the bell seized her attention. Only it was Liam.

'Oh, it's you…'

He swaggered his way to the counter and pulled up a stool. 'Don't sound so disappointed.'

She shook her head. 'I was just expecting someone else. So, did you enjoy playing last night?'

He chuckled then turned to Kris. 'I'll have a double shot flat white thanks.'

'I like a man who knows what he wants,' she said with a decided nod, before winking at Wren. 'Don't you?'

Again, Wren's mouth fell dry. She glanced at her watch then up at the woodchopper cuckoo clock. Clare was late.

'You know, I might have a coffee while I wait too,' Wren said. 'Latte, thanks.'

Kris nodded. 'No problem. You'll be waiting…'

Chapter 12

After waiting an hour for Clare, Wren resolved to walk back to Harenburg Hill to continue writing her sermon. The only problem being that she had left her Bible at the farmhouse.

'I'm sure they have plenty of perfectly good Bibles in the church,' Liam said slyly as they walked.

'I know they do, but mine is… broken-in.'

He grinned. 'Uh-huh.'

'What?'

'Nothing, I just never realised how short you are.'

She laughed. 'What has that got to do with anything?'

'Seriously though,' he said as they continued down Main Street. 'I think this is the first time I've seen you without heels.'

'Well, after my week's grace, I decided to invest in some boots. From the general store, no less,' she said proudly. 'On sale for twenty bucks.'

'Bargain.'

'I know!'

'They suit you…'

There it was again. That tension that had hung between them over their pub dinner. Right before Liam decided to choose Zoe over talking to her.

'Hey, you still there?' Liam asked.

'Hmm? Yeah it's just…'

'What? What have I done this time?'

'No, it's nothing like that.' She stared at the dusty road as they began their walk uphill. 'It's just… why ask me to call you if you had no intention of being in your room?'

'I was in my room.'

'What?' Images of him serenading Zoe suddenly polluted her mind. She blinked them away and stared up at him.

'I didn't want to explain in the café, but that pub food can be a bit dodgy. It gave me an off stomach.'

'What?!' Wren almost laughed. 'You mean to say...'

'I was on the toilet when you called,' he said, defeated.

Wren smirked. 'I see.'

'I never want to see a steak again... I told Zoe as much this morning before I left to find you. I could tell by your message something was up.'

'You could?'

'And then I told her I didn't have any interest in playing at the pub.' He shrugged. 'Besides, the only other songs I know how to play are Christian and I doubted she wanted any of those.'

'What did she say?'

'She said she'd come to church to hear me play then.'

Wren paused mid-step. 'She what?'

'Yeah, I meant to mention it earlier.'

'*You* want to play at Harenburg Hill?'

'Why not?' He shrugged. 'It's got pretty good acoustics. And my guitar was in the boot of my car, as it turns out.'

'Of course, it was.'

'And I'm really missing leading worship.'

'Of course, you are.'

'And I figured, since you don't have a song leader as such, just that funeral organist…'

'Well, *I* like the idea,' Wren said as she unlocked her front door. 'I should probably run it past the elders first though—'

She froze.

'What is it?' Liam asked. 'What's wrong? I don't have to if it'll cause…'

Wren stared at the piece of paper on the hardwood floors. Two slithers of a verse were glued to its centre.

Liam yanked the door open again and burst onto the porch, narrowing his eyes as he searched the country scene.

'In broad daylight,' Wren whispered.

'I'll call the sergeant,' he said, slamming the door behind him again and marching to the kitchen.

She dared not touch it. Instead she knelt before it and read the haunting words only someone with a depraved mind would pull from Holy Scripture and morph into a threat. *Then Amnon hated her with intense hatred.'* The second piece read: *'Amnon said to her, "Get up and get out!"*

'The sergeant is on his way now,' Liam said, kneeling beside Wren and folding her in his arms.

She flinched when he first touched her and continued to stare at the words: *"Get up and get out!"*

Liam pressed his forehead against her. 'Dear Heavenly Father, we pray for your protection once more. Please grant the sergeant wisdom. And please Lord, surround this house with Your angels. We pray for Your peace that transcends all understanding to be over Wren. Protect her and keep her. In Jesus' name, amen.'

'Amen,' Wren whispered.

'I don't care what you say,' Liam said through gritted teeth. 'I'm sleeping on your couch tonight.'

Wren struggled to find her words. She wanted to thank him and dismiss his offer at the same time – although, she knew all too well it wasn't really an offer. It was a statement. So instead, she said, 'I still have work to do.'

'It can wait.'

Slowly, she staggered to her feet. 'What about you?'

'What about me?'

'You've already missed one Sunday. Don't you have to get back?'

His dark eyes stared at her and somehow, she knew what he was going to say even before he opened his mouth. 'I'm not going back.'

Tears seeped down her cheeks. She wanted to be in those arms again. Only the moment was interrupted by a knocking on the door.

'I'll get it,' Liam said.

Wren nodded and shrunk back to the couch to regain her composure.

Armed with a camera and disposable gloves, the sergeant began his work. Wren and Liam offered their statements – which weren't all that in depth considering.

'The other night,' the sergeant began, 'you were sure you locked your front door, weren't you?'

'Yes sir,' Wren replied, feeling like a student in the principal's office. 'I'm not from around here, Sergeant. Where I come from everyone locks their doors. In fact, most have alarms and security cameras.'

He nodded thoughtfully. 'I only ask because whoever it is obviously had a key. There was no sign of forced entry and now they've resolved to sliding their notes under the door.'

'But who would have a key besides Margery Jones and Reverend Williamson?'

'Well, I understand the reverend was moved to a home before he went in for surgery. Are you sure the property was vacant in his absence?'

'I couldn't say,' Wren admitted. 'But I'm sure Kris at the café would know. She knows everything.'

'I'll do some digging and stay in town tonight, just in case,' the sergeant said decidedly. 'Mr Smith, are you able to stay with the reverend this evening?'

'Providing it doesn't get around town by morning.' Liam smirked. 'Right, Wren?'

'We would certainly appreciate your discretion, Sergeant,' Wren said simply.

'It's part of my job description, Reverend,' he said with a kind smile. 'I'll get a room at the pub tonight.'

'Whatever you do, don't have the steak,' Liam said.

'I'm a fish and chips man, myself,' he replied. 'I'll come back and see you both in the morning.'

Chapter 13

While Liam was on the phone to the eldership at Living Hope, Wren was trying to work through her sermon. But the verse from 2 Samuel kept plaguing her mind… *'intense hatred'*… *"Get up, and get out!"*… It had to be a man. Both verses showed a man hurting a woman in some way. Wren remembered young Frank Sutherland's brooding eyes in the front row, evidently hating every moment of sitting there. She remembered him stomping past her without so much as a glance. Then she remembered Ava unable to take her attention away from the front pews and the way she had lost all sense of composure when Wren had simply mentioned the name 'Sutherland'. No wonder they didn't want Ava hanging around and forced her out. There was more to it. After all, if Ava was attacked by some random passer through, then surely the church would help her through that horror. Unless they themselves had something to hide.

Wren jumped as a desperate knock thudded on the front door.

'I gotta go,' Liam said before slamming the phone into place. He glanced at Wren and placed a finger to his lips to hush her. He then pointed and she followed his direction and stayed in the kitchen.

Another desperate knock.

From the kitchen, Wren could hear Liam lift the latch.

'Who is it?' he demanded.

A small voice replied, far too small for Wren to even recognise it. She peered around the archway while Liam eagerly unlocked the door.

Clare stood in the warm glow of the porch sconces, blood gleaming from her forehead. There were no tears, but her blouse was torn open. Her hair was up like a bird's nest, as though someone had taken a fistful of it.

Wren gasped.

Clare stumbled inside and into Wren's open arms.

Slowly, Liam closed the door and returned to the kitchen. Wren could hear his faint voice, but it seemed nothing in comparison to Clare's rasping breaths.

'He found my pills,' she whispered, staring blankly ahead.

Wren guided Clare to the couch and set her down.

'Sergeant's around the corner,' Liam said.

Wren nodded. 'Water?'

Within a moment, Liam returned with not one but two glasses. Wren reached for the first and put it to Clare's lips which responded sluggishly, allowing water to run down her chin and dilute the blood that clung there.

'And he wonders why I was taking them to begin with,' she went on.

Wren didn't want to ask but knew her duty to this woman all too well. 'Did Sean do this to you?'

Clare blinked then stared at the floor.

'What pills did he find, Clare?' Wren asked, though she was terrified of the answer. She'd had too many run-ins with drugs in her time. She knew their effects. She had been a bystander to them most of her childhood.

'Contraceptive,' Clare eventually muttered. 'I've been on them for years. Ever since the first time he—'

Wren clasped Clare's hand in her own. 'It's okay…'

Clare's bloodshot eyes rolled in Wren's direction. 'I didn't want to bring a child into this.'

Wren nodded slowly as blue and red lights flashed from beyond the window. 'You're safe now.'

Clare cringed. 'I just want to get cleaned up.'

'Just wait for the sergeant.'

When the sergeant entered the living room, Wren dutifully stepped back and allowed him to approach Clare with the same gentle bedside manner he had used with her.

'I just want to shower,' Clare sobbed after a few minutes and began to scratch at the dried blood on her arm.

The sergeant briefly studied the photos on his digital camera. His face drained to white. 'That's fine,' he said. 'You go on.'

Clare struggled to her feet.

Wren stepped forward only to be dismissed with a flaccid wave. 'Well, the bathroom's—'

'I know where it is,' Clare replied.

The sergeant stood to attention. '*How?*'

Clare sighed, lingering by the doorway. 'What do you mean?'

'How do you know where the bathroom is? Do you come to this house often?'

'I...' She glanced between them, her eyes shining with unadulterated fear. 'I...'

'It's okay,' Wren said, closing in. 'Just tell us how you know?'

Her mouth twisted from side to side as she seemingly debated with herself. 'The church let me stay here last time this...' She gestured to her face and released a breathy sad laugh. 'I was going to leave him. The place was vacant at the time... No one was meant to know.'

'Kris wouldn't have known that,' she said in undertones to the sergeant.

He simply shook his head. 'Can you tell us what happened to the key that was in your possession?'

'Sean said he gave it back to the church.'

'Your husband?'

She nodded weakly. 'Can I have a shower now?'

'In a moment,' he said, looking curiously at her. 'Were there ever times when your husband was unaccounted for? When he didn't come home?'

'Of course,' she said without hesitation.

The sergeant continued to nod. 'Did he give you a reason?'

'I learned not to ask, but it wouldn't surprise me if…' Her mouth folded in on itself. 'Are you going to arrest him, Sergeant?'

'Yes. So you can finish your sentence.'

'It's hearsay.'

'Regardless, it could help my case.'

Clare looked to Wren.

'Please,' Wren said, 'please tell him everything you know.'

Clare rested a bloodied hand on the doorframe. 'There was a rumour he knocked up that girl.' She cringed. 'That young pretty one from the café. But of course, my father-in-law put a quick end to that one.'

'Ava?' Wren whispered.

'Can I please have a shower?'

The sergeant gave a single nod then continued to write in his notebook. 'If you ask me, Reverend, I believe it's a one culprit fits all situation.'

Wren bit her lip. 'What do you know about the younger brother, Frank Sutherland?'

'I know he moved back home after a similar thing happened to Judith,' the sergeant said, nodding in the direction of the hallway. 'All charges were dropped, of course. Poor bloke is bitter as all hell, but he wouldn't hurt a fly. Unlike others in his family, evidently.'

'I see.'

Liam wrapped his arm around her shoulders. 'Why are you curious about the brother?'

Wren shook her head. 'Because just like the rest of this town, I've been judging someone unfairly.'

The sergeant offered a weak smile. 'If you'd excuse me, Reverend. I'm going to find Sean Sutherland and take him to the station.'

'I'll walk you out,' Liam said.

Once alone, Wren fell to her knees.

Chapter 14

Wren approached the pulpit the following Sunday morning weak and deflated. Her throat was hoarse, her sinuses ached, and her body felt like it had been hit by a semi-truck. For the first time, the Sutherlands were nowhere to be seen and, after strict instruction from the eldership, she refrained from explaining their absence to the now three-dozen members of Harenburg Hill.

'This may not seem customary,' Wren croaked into the microphone, sounding every bit the man the congregation wished she were. 'But I would like to invite Liam Smith to bless us in song.'

There was silence.

Liam carried his guitar to the pulpit – the only microphone at the ready – and began to strum. Rather than returning to her seat, Wren went to sit beside Margery Jones, since her row was half emptied.

'Don't worry,' Wren whispered. 'It's beautiful.'

Margery glanced sideways at her, but her lips remained pursed.

'Gospel centred,' Wren added. 'And he *is* a man, after all.'

'The only thing I'm worried about is catching that ghastly cold,' Margery returned sharply. 'If I were your mother, I'd send you to bed with lemon tea and not let you out.'

Her words startled Wren into silence and she subtly shifted to leave a small space between them. Wren smiled to herself. *'If I were your mother…'*

Wren then returned her attention to the stage where Liam's soulful voice was sure to penetrate any heart of stone. With the lyrics of praise he had written with his own pen, he lifted his voice to heaven. And Wren, like many others in the congregation, couldn't contain her tears.

'I can't believe you sat next to the Queen Mother,' Kris said as she exited the church that Sunday. She took hold of Wren's arm and began to walk downhill.

Wren glanced back over her shoulder. 'I'm meant to be saying goodbye to people,' she protested. 'I'm meant to shake their hands...'

'Since when do any of them shake *your* hand?'

'You're a bad influence. I'm a reverend!'

'Well, maybe Margery would've shaken your hand today. Since it seems she has gotten over her ridiculous jealousy.'

Wren came to a standstill. 'What did you just say?'

'Sorry, Reverend,' Kris said, almost seriously. 'I didn't mean to be disrespectful.'

'No, I mean.' Wren shook her head. 'Why would Margery be jealous of me? She despises me?'

'Only because you have the life she always wanted. Or at least, the life Margery Forsyth always wanted,' Kris said, squinting up at her. 'You really had no idea?'

Wren's mouth gaped.

'The Forsyth Reverends of Harenburg Hill? Her great-grandfather, her grandfather, her father, all ministers…' Kris seemed to be waiting for Wren to catch on, until she finally blurted, 'Poor girl couldn't understand why she couldn't be the next in succession, as it were. Then you show up thirty-odd years later when all her best years are behind her and she's stuck under a patriarchal eldership with the laughable responsibility of taking notes in their meetings.'

Wren looked back up at Harenburg Hill. 'I have to talk to her…'

'And embarrass her even more?' Kris shook her head. 'No, what you *have* to do is include her.'

'Really? That's it?'

'Wren,' Kris said in a genuinely serious tone. 'It's all she has ever wanted.'

'Right… thanks.'

'So?' Kris prodded.

'Mmm?'

'What are you waiting for?'

Wren nodded once. 'Right.' Then she marched back up to Harenburg Hill just in time to see the limited members of the front row.

'Lovely music,' Peter said, reaching out to shake Wren's hand as she approached. 'Perhaps your friend, Mr Smith, would be available to lead the congregation occasionally?'

'I'm sure he'd love that.'

'Yes, well,' Trevor Burns began until he caught sight of Rosemary. 'Must go. Good job…'

Donald watched after him, his bushy brows drawn together. 'What's got into that bloke?'

'Mrs Jones,' Wren began, extending her hand and hoping the gesture wouldn't be in vain. 'I was wondering if we might have a word inside, unless you have to rush off?'

'Are you contagious?' she asked cautiously.

'Probably,' Wren said, 'but I could really use your opinion with an issue, but it requires the utmost discretion.'

Margery Jones' lips remained pursed, but her eyes ignited with the faintest flame. With a gloved hand, she reached out and shook Wren's bare hand once, then drew back again. 'I suppose I can spare a few moments. Shall I wait in your office?'

'Yes, please.'

Margery turned toward Harenburg Hill, her nose slightly higher than it was before. 'Oh,' she said, catching Liam's arm on his way out. 'Well done. You really must start leading the worship. If the reverend approves, of course.'

Wren's eyes rounded.

Liam grinned. 'I'll be happy to convince her.'

Margery's cheeks flushed. 'Well, I've said my piece…'

'High praise, indeed,' Wren said once Margery was safely inside.

'Don't take this personally, but you sound awful,' Liam said.

'Believe me, I feel it, too.'

'Please tell me you're going straight home.'

'Soon,' she said. 'First I need to deal with a few issues.'

'Sounds ominous.'

Wren nodded slowly. 'Let's just say, things are changing.'

In the depths of the offices of Harenburg Hill, there were now only two people remaining

– Wren and Margery Jones. As Wren entered her office, she caught Margery straightening, adjusting herself in one of the guest chairs. Wren removed her sash and robe and hung them on the spare chair. Margery watched with interest.

'Well,' she said when Wren finally joined her, 'what can I do for you?'

Wren leaned her forearms on the desk and looked Margery in the eye. 'There is a sensitive subject I have to discuss with you. It's about the Sutherlands.'

Margery's tone softened. 'I'm aware of Sean's current... *predicament*.'

'Do you know why he's in jail?'

'Well, he's only at the station,' Margery corrected. 'At this stage, as I understand, they don't have enough proof for some of the convictions and he may be released on bail.'

Wren slumped back into her chair. 'So, you know all this? You know what he did to Clare?'

'I *heard* what he did to Clare. From Judith's mouth, mind. I'm no gossip.'

Wren gazed at her for a long moment. 'Would you like some chocolate?'

Margery's manicured brows leapt upward. 'Sorry?'

'Never mind. Back to the Sutherlands, I think we need to have an eldership meeting to discuss the issue and how we are going to handle it.'

'There's nothing to handle,' she said. 'Neil Sutherland has the bail money, as I understand Clare has been staying with you...'

'Yes, but it's all band-aids and brushing it under the rug. This is a serious issue.' Wren's voice almost broke as she remembered the sight of Clare in her living room. 'One of our church members has been abused by her husband for years, a trait he has evidently picked up from his father who just so happens to be an elder of Harenburg Hill. Now, I'm hoping, as a fellow woman, you can see the value of dealing with this situation sensitively but thoroughly. Do you have any suggestions?'

Margery folded her hands in her lap. 'Well, if you ask me, Neil Sutherland stepping down from the eldership is a non-negotiable.'

'Great,' Wren said, scribbling it down on her notebook.

'And I suppose we should ensure Clare has the appropriate support, so she isn't bullied into dropping charges.'

'Yes…'

'And perhaps, you should speak to that young girl at the café,' Margery said, somewhat quieter. 'I don't think she understands what she's in the middle of.'

Wren slowly nodded.

'And the members of the church really should be informed of Neil Sutherland's change in position. Formally. No rumours, just facts.'

Wren continued to scribble. 'Anything else?'

'Yes, actually,' she said with her usual grace and poise. 'Perhaps, we need to start paying our reverend sick leave.'

Wren closed her notebook. 'If you insist.'

'At least, I understand the miscommunication now.' Margery rose from her seat. 'You really do sound like a man.'

'Well, thank you for your help.'

'Mmm-hmm,' was Margery Jones' reply. Though as she left the office, Wren was sure she saw a bounce in her step.

Chapter 15

After a restless night, Wren woke with a throbbing head and an anxious heart. This was the day of the eldership meeting. She was determined to let all the members have their say — except for old Neil Sutherland of course, who she sincerely hoped didn't show. Fortunately, she had her bodyguard on standby. Liam was in the church kitchen making some of his famous chicken noodle soup.

'Is there anything that man can't do?' Margery asked as she took her usual seat in the front pew.

'If there is, I haven't found it yet,' Wren said with a grin.

'Imagine if Neil was here.' Trevor shook his head. 'What he'd say to a man being in the kitchen?' He chuckled but for lack of company his amusement was short lived.

Wren curled her leg beneath her as she tried to get comfortable on the hardwood chair. 'Well, we have a matter to discuss along those lines, however, first I'd like to open it up to any other items?'

'May I just say, Reverend, you look mighty uncomfortable on that chair,' Donald said with a cheesy grin.

Wren looked sideways at him. 'I assure you, I'm perfectly fine. So any suggestions before we get started? Anyone?'

'These pews really do hurt the old back,' Donald went on.

Now, he had the attention of the room. Wren was waiting for Margery to explode but Donald continued.

'Imagine,' he said, fanning his hand before them. 'Instead of pews, we have cushioned chairs.' He allowed the suggestion to hang in the air for a long moment before adding, 'No more discomfort. No more turning in from the edge of the pew. We could arrange them in a *curve*. Very ergonomic!'

'Wouldn't a curve take up more room?' Trevor asked.

'Well, yes, but just think of the perks. Comfort! And safety! Those pews really are a fire hazard…'

'Harenburg Hill has always had pews and will always have pews,' Margery said decidedly. 'First, you'll change the aesthetics and next thing you know we'll have a drum kit and neon lights.'

'It does seem like an unnecessary expense,' agreed Peter.

'Or an investment?' Donald's eyes lit up. 'Just imagine, clearing the chairs away during the week so we could hire out the hall. Birthdays, weddings, Bar Mitzvahs…'

Margery tutted. 'Oh, so we're Jewish now?'

'We could even have *assisted* chairs for us elderly folk.'

'Speak for yourself,' Trevor scoffed.

'Reverend?' Donald asked. 'Any thoughts?'

Wren was dumbfounded. She didn't know people could have such firm convictions about chairs. 'Perhaps,' she began, glancing between dear Donald and his opposition, 'perhaps we could bring it up at the next member's meeting? Since the congregation use the chairs as well.'

'The pews,' Margery corrected.

'Yes, of course. The pews…'

'That sounds fair,' Donald agreed.

Wren glanced at her watch. She was feeling weary and they were running out of time. 'Well, if no one has any other business—'

Donald, Trevor, and Peter automatically began to rise from their evidently uncomfortable pews, but Margery stopped them with a single glare.

'I'm not finished,' Wren said.

They returned to their seats.

'As I was saying, if no one has any other business, I would like to discuss the Sutherland family situation.'

'Oh, that's really none of our business,' Donald said, preparing to stand again.

'An elder of this church is seemingly beating his wife and indivertibly teaching his son to do the same, and you think it's none of our business?' Wren blurted.

'Well,' Peter said, 'I suppose if you put it like that.'

'I thought Judith dropped any charges,' Trevor added.

'Well, what about Clare? Shall I show you the photos of her bleeding and bruised, or do you believe me?'

The men fell silent.

'It's only appropriate that Neil Sutherland resign from his position at Harenburg Hill,' Margery said. 'I spoke to Reverend Williamson and he's on the mend, though still in hospital. Once he returns, we'll have another member of the eldership.'

'He's not in hospital,' Peter said quietly.

'Of course, he is. I spoke to him this morning,' Margery replied.

'I planned to visit yesterday afternoon,' Peter said. 'No one at the city hospital had heard of him.'

'He has been bed ridden for almost a month,' Margery argued. 'How can they say—'

'There's just no record.' Peter shrugged. 'I got them to spell it every way I could think of and sure enough, no George Williamson on their books. Not since his heart attack five years ago. Oh, but I wasn't meant to know that…'

'Then where is the old fella then?' Donald asked.

'We're digressing,' Wren reminded them.

'No, we're not,' Trevor argued. 'He was our reverend first. We need to know what happened to him. Suppose he died on the operating table?'

Margery gritted her teeth. 'I spoke to him this morning…'

'Maybe he's actually gone to some shonky black-market surgeon because it's cheaper?' Donald said. 'Reverends don't make that much.' He nodded to Wren. 'No offence.'

She smiled weakly. 'Believe me, I'm only in this line of work because of God's grace.'

'Do we file a missing person's report?' Peter asked.

Margery Jones rose to her feet. 'No one will do anything of the sort. The next time I speak to him, I will straighten it out. In the meantime, I believe we should schedule a member's meeting to inform them of the changes within the eldership and to discuss those blasted chairs!'

'Pews,' Donald corrected, 'those blasted pews.'

'Now, Reverend,' Margery said, scaling her voice down by a few decibels. 'I really think you ought to go home. That sick leave we discussed is being enforced as of today.'

Chapter 16

Under Margery Jones' strict instruction, Wren returned to the farmhouse – locking the door behind her – and went up to bed. Still, she couldn't sleep. She couldn't help but play Margery's words over in her head, that Neil Sutherland was willing and able to pay the bail money to free Sean. She didn't know how to tell Clare, who had been staying in the spare room of the farmhouse since the incident. At least, Wren felt safer with someone in the house. That was, until a rock came through her window that night sheathed in a piece of paper.

'Are you okay?' Clare called, her bare feet slapping their way down the hall.

Wren leapt out of bed, staring at the shards of glass and the intruding object. *Please Lord, protect us…*

Another crash came from downstairs. Was it the back door? Wren and Clare shared an uncertain look shrouded in fear.

'Is the only phone downstairs?' Clare whispered.

Wren slowly nodded and took her Bible from the nightstand. Clutching it to her belly, she neared the bedroom doorway. Meanwhile, Clare carefully tiptoed over the glass and unwrapped the scrunched paper. Wren glanced over. Another verse. *'Look, I am coming soon! My reward is with me, and I will give to each person according to what they have done.'*

'Revelation,' Wren whispered.

Clare stared up at her.

Wren's fingers tightened around God's Word. 'Stay here.'

She knew she wouldn't have to tell Clare twice. After all, Clare knew firsthand what Sean was capable of. The sergeant just didn't have enough evidence, and without a confession or witnesses it was a hopeless case. The hardwoods creaked as Wren slowly made her way toward the kitchen, her steps as light as she could manage. The farmhouse was dim except for the porch lights but Wren felt as though she glowed in the dark in her white nightie. She slid along the hallway wall, careful not to make a sound, conscious of the Bible in her hands. Somehow it felt warm. Perhaps it was just her own sweaty palms, but she preferred to believe God made it so to comfort her. If only Liam was here, but last she heard he was putting the finishing touches on his soup. He promised he would come to check on her. He promised he would bring some soup to help her recover. He promised, once upon a time, that she was the woman God told him to marry and that he would always love and protect her. Still, when she needed him, where was he?

I will never leave you or forsake you, a voice whispered from deep within her conscious.

Wren nodded slowly, concentrating on the warmth of the Bible pressed against her stomach. Her heart thudded as she tiptoed to the landline. She was sure the last number dialled was the sergeant. All she had to do was hit redial. That was it. She just had to get to that button. She pressed herself against the wall, forehead to the doorframe, and quietly picked up the receiver—

But a gloved hand smothered her mouth from behind.

Her muffled scream was barely audible. She reached for the burnt orange button in vain.

'You just couldn't help yourself, could you?' the man hissed, dragging her backwards.

Her Bible tumbled from her hands as she writhed, pulling at the man's black-cladded arms. She screamed as hard as she could, but she barely made a sound. She began to slap her feet on the hardwoods as she was dragged into the living room. He pressed her down, face first into the cushions. Wren's body exploded with fear. Every inch of her trembled and shivered and fought. She could scarcely breathe through her blocked nose. She could feel her lungs waning. His hand was still firm on her mouth as he straddled her from behind, forcing her face deeper into the cushions before drawing it up by clumps of her hair to taunt her.

'I told you to get out. You just don't listen do you, you little...'

Wren's limbs burned as she writhed against the harsh fabric. Her face scratched against it as he forced her down again, one hand over her mouth and the other firm against her hair. Bird's nest hair. As her head grew light, she remembered Clare's face that night. Suddenly, it all made sense. He had just meant to intimidate her. It was an effort he had put into the beating. *This* was different. This was just the quickest means to an end.

In one last attempt of defence, Wren swung her head and bit down on the gloved hand as hard as her jaw would allow. He growled, forcing her to turn over beneath him before whacking her across the cheek. A sting followed by throbbing. Her head flew sideways but her eyes rolled up to look at him.

Sean's stare burned into her with intense hatred.

'Please…'

'Shut up!' he screeched, saliva spraying from his mouth. He wrapped both hands around her neck. She kicked her legs, her aching fingers pried at his solid grasp.

She coughed. 'Please… don't…'

As Wren began to lose consciousness, another crash resonated from afar. As her eyes drifted closed, she felt the weight of Sean's body fall on her. Her breaths were weak and shallow. Her neck burned. She could still taste the leather of his glove. She could smell hot blood. Was it his or hers? She didn't know. She couldn't feel enough to know if she was bleeding for fear had ignited her body. She had to fight against it just to open her eyes.

Blood. She could see it now. Clumping Sean's once fair hair.

And Clare stood over him, an ornate solid brass lamp in her hands. Quivering. She panted as she stood in shock.

'What's going on in there?' Liam shouted, banging on the front door.

Clare and Wren remained unmoved.

So did Sean.

Wren could hear Liam kicking the door and it soon gave way. He burst into the dimly lit room, horror straining his face.

'I'm okay,' Wren whispered, knowing it was the very thing he needed to hear even if it was far from true.

His face twisted as his eyes glazed over. Within two strides, he was at her side, easing Sean's flaccid body from her.

'Call an ambulance,' he said to Clare.

Slowly, she began to nod and lowered the lamp.

Liam cupped Wren's face in his hands. 'Are you sure you're okay?'

She cringed. Tears seeped from her eyes and she slowly shook her head. She looked down at her white nightie, stained with Sean's blood. Her hands instinctively swiped at it, wishing it to disappear.

'Hey,' he said, taking hold of her hands and pulling her into him. 'Come here. You're safe now.'

Chapter 17

By the time Wren returned to Harenburg Hill – with full health, thanks to the power of prayer and Liam's chicken noodle soup – the elders had already taken it upon themselves to inform the four-dozen church members of the Sutherland family situation. No rumours. Just facts. With Sean in prison and old Neil Sutherland leaving the township of Brite, there was now only Judith and young Frank who remained. Clare may have only been an honorary member of the Sutherland clan but nevertheless Judith took her in, allowing her youngest son to finally have his freedom. Which was why Wren was surprised to see Frank waiting in her office with two cups of takeaway coffee.

'Hi Reverend,' he said, rising from the chair.

It was the most words he had ever spoken to her. She paused, somewhat taken aback as she stood there casually in her t-shirt and jeans. She certainly didn't feel like a 'reverend' today. She didn't even have her heels to give her an extra boost, as she had taken to walking around town.

'Good morning Frank,' she said, veering around the desk. 'What can I do for you this morning?'

'Latte, right,' he said, sliding one cup across the desk, flashing his complete sleeve of tattoos on his right arm.

'Yeah, right… thanks.' She took her first sip and sighed.

He took a gulp of his, finishing off with an 'ah'.

Wren gazed down at the biodegradable cup. 'Frank, I owe you an apology.'

'Nah, you don't.'

'Yes,' she said decidedly. 'I may not have said anything but in my head I was judging you and I thought you were behind a lot of what was going on. And I had no reason to. It wasn't fair.'

'I reckon I gave you a reason,' he said with a chuckle. 'I was moody as all hell every week. It probably looked like I hated ya.'

'Well, yeah, maybe but—'

'Look, Reverend,' he said, leaning both his colourful arms on the desk. 'I have a favour to ask ya.'

'What?'

'Ava and I would like your blessing to get married,' Frank said.

Coffee spurted from Wren's mouth. 'Sorry, what?!'

Frank shifted back slightly but his stare remained on her. 'I'm serious. We would like to get married at Harenburg Hill. And we'd like for you to marry us, if ya don't have anything against it.'

'What…' Wren reached for a tissue and dabbed her mouth. 'What about… the baby?' she said quietly. 'Doesn't that bother you?'

''Course, it *bothers* me,' he said. 'Why do you think I want to make an honest woman out of her? It was *one* time. We tried not to. But it was one time. Honestly, Reverend, I swear on—'

Wren raised her hand. 'I believe you, it's okay.' She took a moment to process. 'So, what you mean to tell me is this whole time the two of you have been lying about it?'

'Not by choice,' Frank said. 'Dad found out and forced us to. He said he'd make Ava's life a living hell otherwise. That he'd never accept her into the family. I should've stuck up for her, but I couldn't leave Mum there. At least Ava was safe with her family.'

'And now that your father has left Brite…'

'Yeah.' He shrugged. 'I know it sounds farfetched, but I really do love her, Reverend.'

'Have you told Kris what you just told me?'

'Ava's explaining this morning.' His lips slipped into a wry grin. 'She's softening the blow with chocolate cake.'

'You guys will need more than that.' Wren released a breathy laugh. 'Have you really thought this through? Marriage is a big commitment.'

Frank didn't hesitate. 'Reverend, once you know you know. And *I* know.'

'Okay, well, providing you still feel this way next week, both of you come and see me. We'll start some marriage lessons.'

His eyes narrowed. 'Marriage lessons?'

'Yeah, we'll just make sure you guys are on the right track.'

'Have *you* ever been married, Reverend?'

A lump formed in her throat and she struggled to voice herself past it. 'No… but I once rejected a proposal because I felt the Holy Spirit pull me in a different direction. It's all about God's calling on your life.'

'Did you regret it after?'

Wren shook her head. 'It was the right thing at the time.'

Frank Sutherland's question remained with her for the rest of the day – did she regret it? If someone had asked her that question the night Sean broke into the farmhouse, she might have said yes. She might have admitted she wished she had stuck to her five-year plan, to work in an associate pastoral role in a church that appreciated her, to marry the sensible Christian man God had placed in her life, and to save money for their perfect wedding. Instead, her decision had launched her into a job role where she had felt unsupported and undermined. She had ultimately dragged Liam away from his dream position to look after her in amongst the chaos. And now, she didn't even know where she stood with him. Sure, he cared about her – she knew he always would – but with her small wage and him leaving his job, the best they could afford would be a mediocre wedding. That was if he still even wanted to marry her at all. Which she doubted. Few men came back from a rejected proposal still fighting. Most simply picked up the pieces of their broken hearts, swiftly and quietly, trying to keep their masculine dignity intact. Then they moved on. Perhaps that was exactly what Wren now needed to do – move on. After all, with her experience, she could probably find a job anywhere. Her key skills would now list working with dysfunctional families, ability to work under threat, and surviving when a member of the church attempts to kill you.

Chapter 18

Insomnia became Wren's companion on a Sunday morning at which time she would take to the porch swing for a time of reflection and prayer before beginning the day.

With plenty of young families now at Harenburg Hill, many came early for tea and coffee in the church kitchen while Wren took the Sunday school lesson in the main hall. Since it was always a simplified version of the sermon, Wren spoke to the children about relationships and being loving toward each other. Considering recent events, she felt it was time to preach a sermon on marriage. Even if the congregation believed her to be underqualified on the subject.

Once again there were a few new faces piled into the pews, most of them taking a moment to appreciate Liam's joyful strumming. None seemed so pleased as an elderly gentleman in a Hawaiian shirt, shorts, and sandals. He beamed as he made his way down the aisle. His eyes shone with a youthfulness long forgotten and his tanned skin, though leathery, glowed with health. His smile was wide as he approached the front pew, shocking the remaining elders.

'Oh!' Margery gasped and dropped the rest of the hymn board numbers, sending them flying like playing cards in a flamboyant party trick. 'Reverend Williamson?!'

Wren froze as she watched Margery make her way down the stage seemingly pleased yet apprehensive at once. In fact, Wren had never seen Margery so taken aback, as though a ghost were standing before her. The strumming came to a halt and before Wren could introduce herself or explain why she was in his place, filling *his* shoes – a woman, no less – she was at the pulpit welcoming the congregation. She glanced his way occasionally. He simply smiled. He had set himself beside the prim and proper eldership to which he looked nothing alike. Wren had imagined a character much like the imposing

Neil Sutherland, but this fit cheerful man hadn't even entered her mind as a possibility.

Wren was grateful to introduce Liam once again, who would lead the congregation in song. So as not to startle everyone with more change, Liam had learnt a few hymns but added his own soulful twist.

'What a friend we have in Jesus,' he began slowly – all he needed was a robed gospel choir behind him voicing their hallelujahs. *'All our sins and griefs to bear-yeah-i-yeah-i-yeah… And what a pri-vi-lege to ca-a-a-a-rr-y-y-y… Every-thing to-o God… in prayer…'* After a pause, his fingers quickened on the strings. *'Oh! Yeah, what peace we often… forfeit… Oh! What needless pain we bear… All because we do not ca-a-a-rr-y-y-y yea-oh-yeah… Everything to God in prayer…'*

As the tempo hastened, Frank in the back row began to clap. Ava smiled up at him, singing and rubbing her protruding belly. Soon others in the congregation caught on and Wren glanced over at Margery Jones. She may have had her same expression of steel, but Wren was sure she could see her kitten heel tapping. As Wren continued to survey the joyful congregants, her

gaze fell upon two faces she did not expect –
Mum and Esther. The latter pulled a face and
gave her two solid thumbs up. Mum simply
smiled at her like only a mother could,
comforting her at once and settling any
apprehension. After all, part of her felt nervous
preaching in front of the esteemed Reverend
George Williamson. Though, she had to admit,
the Hawaiian shirt had taken some of the edge
off already.

When it was her turn to approach the
pulpit, she didn't climb the stairs. Instead she
slowly removed her sash and robe and laid them
down. She took her old broken-in Word of God,
the one that had followed her across the state
and had stayed with her that night in the
farmhouse, offering its protective warmth. She
set herself on the edge of the stage then kicked
off her heels.

The congregation remained silent. And
Reverend George Williamson? Well, he was still
smiling.

'I had a sermon planned for today,' Wren
said, 'but somehow it doesn't seem relevant
anymore... So I would just like to read you some

verses the Lord placed on my heart when I first came to Harenburg Hill. If you could please turn in your Bibles to 2 Corinthians chapter three.'

Wren glanced at the old reverend again. He was looking around the room, watching the people find their way in God's Word, his smile remaining all the while.

'Are we beginning to commend ourselves again?' She read aloud. *'Or do we need, like some people, letters of recommendation to you or from you?'* She swallowed hard. *'You yourselves are our letter, written on our hearts, known and read by everyone. You show that you are a letter from Christ, the result of our ministry, written not with ink but with the Spirit of the living God, not on tablets of stone but on tablets of human hearts...'* Wren briefly wet her lips before adding, 'That was my prayer for this church.' She paused, focusing on the single word spinning around in her head: *was.* 'So, I'd now like to invite Reverend George Williamson forward, if he would like to address his congregation,' she said with a weak smile. 'As you can see, he's the picture of health.'

Collecting her shoes and Bible, Wren returned to her seat beside Liam.

Happily, George Williamson marched onto the stage, his smile unwavering. He cleared his throat then leaned deeply into the microphone and announced: 'I knew she'd be good for you lot.'

Wren's brow furrowed and she looked over to the front pew. Margery looked just as confused. And if Margery didn't know anything, then no one did.

'When I saw this young lady's CV, I forwarded it straight to Trevor and said *this* is my replacement. Do what it takes to get *him*, on board.' Reverend Williamson grinned. 'Yeah, sorry about that, Trev. I only found out myself after I checked her references.' He looked to Wren, 'Yeah, I may or may not have told the eldership not to bother with that themselves. I wanted them to offer you the position.'

Wren's Bible almost slipped straight off her lap.

'I just didn't know how to get through to us,' he went on, 'and I was exhausted of trying. I knew there was some funny business going on behind closed doors, but no one would admit anything.' He shrugged. 'I've been doing this job for over thirty years and I'm bloody tired.'

There were a few sniggers from the congregation, but Margery Jones hadn't lost her look of horror.

'I even had to fake a health scare just to go on holiday,' he said. 'By the way, go to Bali. You don't know what you're missing.'

This time, even Wren smirked.

'When I read Wren's...' He cleared his throat again. 'Apologies let me start again. When I read *Reverend* Wren Finley's sermons, I knew she would bring something special to this place. I'd given up on writing my own years ago and no one even noticed. Seriously, I even preached one two weeks in a row just to check and no one thought I was going senile...'

Margery Jones' face finally softened into a small smile.

'Reverend,' he said, looking straight at Wren. 'This isn't *my* congregation anymore. God's called *you* to be its shepherd. If you're willing?'

Chapter 19

Sunday lunch at the farmhouse consisted of Liam's roast lamb and Wren's frozen winter vegetables – even though it was barely autumn. Still, a cool change lingered on the horizon that nipped at night then slipped away like the tide during the day. Her early mornings on the porch would soon have to come to an end, unless she wanted hypothermia. Everyone warned her how cold Brite became in winter. Maybe it was time for her to fly south? Still, for now, the days were at least warm enough to eat lunch on the back porch.

'Living Hope just isn't the same without you two,' Esther said brightly as she spooned mint jelly onto her plate.

'Way to guilt trip,' Liam muttered.

'When are you coming home anyway?'

Mum cleared her throat. 'Could someone please pass me the gravy?'

Liam took the jug and angled the handle toward her. 'Here.'

'I guess, for me, I'll just have to pray about it,' Wren said.

Liam returned to his lunch in silence.

'Well, it kinda involves Liam, too...' Esther pulled her mouth sideways. 'Awkward...'

Wren looked to Liam, who continued to stare at his plate. 'Could you please help me get some drinks from the kitchen?'

'Oh, I can help with that,' Esther said, practically leaping from her seat.

'No, you're a guest here,' Liam said softly and took hold of Wren's hand.

Once inside and out of hearing, Wren leaned against the peppermint cabinetry and watched as Liam retrieved juice from the fridge.

'You didn't tell her, did you?' Wren asked softly.

'There was no point,' Liam said, leaning to find the mineral water.

'Didn't you think she would find out eventually?'

Liam placed the drinks on the laminate benchtop followed by four glasses. After closer inspection, he ran the tap and rinsed off the dust. He then placed them on a tea towel and finally turned to face her, leaning against the wide ceramic sink.

Wren shifted uncomfortably and averted her attention.

'Look at me,' he whispered.

'Mmm?'

'Do you still *not* know?'

Her breath caught in her chest and she had to remind herself to exhale again. Why did he suddenly make her so nervous?

'Why did you call me that night?' he asked. 'You could've called your mum or anyone.'

Wren thought back to that moment – slumped against the door of her office, clinging to the phone long after he had lost reception. He was the only one she wanted to call. Because he was the one she needed. After God, he was her next emergency contact. He was the person she wanted to rely on, even if that made her vulnerable. And she didn't even comprehend it until that day on the phone when she realised how much she missed him.

'Because something changed on the phone that day,' she said softly. 'We laughed and… and flirted… a bit… I don't remember us ever being like that until Harenburg Hill. It was all seriousness and planning…'

'You love planning.'

'I love spontaneity, too,' she argued. 'And romance…'

'Hey, I tried that day. It wasn't my fault God made it rain.'

Wren smirked. 'It wasn't the rain. It was us.'

Liam crossed the space between them, looming over her. 'And now?'

'Now, I'm scared,' she whispered.

'Why?'

'Because I don't just want to go back to a perfect five-year plan.'

'What about if we change it to an imperfect lifetime plan?' he said, leaning closer. 'A lifetime of laughing. A lifetime of flirting…'

'A lifetime of chicken noodle soup?'

He chuckled. 'Everyday if you want it.'

'Well, that might be a bit mu—'

Liam leaned way down and pressed his lips to hers. Wren's head spun as she shifted up onto her tiptoes and wrapped her arms around his neck for something to hold onto. After an eternal moment, he slowly tugged away and gazed down at her with those deep onyx eyes.

'Does that mean we're staying?' Wren whispered.

Liam chuckled. 'Wrenley, it has nothing to with whether we're staying or leaving. That's between us and God. He'll tell us what to do.'

'We would both earn more money at Living Hope,' she said, suddenly picturing wedding dresses and floral arrangements.

'That's true, it would set us up nicely…'

'I sense a "but" coming?'

'*But* money isn't everything.' He shrugged. 'Maybe I was never meant to be a pastor. I certainly enjoy leading worship more than I do preaching sermons.'

She gazed up at him curiously. 'Then why would God send you to Bible college?'

'To meet you, of course,' he said softly and kissed her again.

This time it was Wren who broke away. 'I think our family is going to start wondering where we are.'

'Oh yeah, *them.*' He turned and piled the bottles of drinks into his arms.

Grinning to herself, Wren then collected the glasses and carried them out back.

'Too late, we ate all the meat,' Esther said with a broad smile.

'Juice or mineral water?' Liam asked.

'Oh, I'll just mix them together,' Esther said. 'Live on the wild side…'

'Mineral water, thank you,' Mum replied before turning her attention to Wren. 'By the smile on your face, I'm guessing you're not coming home?'

Esther's face dropped. 'What?! How did I miss the smile?'

'We're going to keep praying about it,' Wren said.

'Does that mean we'll have to drive all the way back for the wedding?' Esther asked.

Wren opened her mouth to speak but nothing came out. How could she explain to Liam's foster sister that she in fact rejected him and didn't even know until five minutes prior where she stood?

Fortunately, Liam stepped in. 'I imagine we'll want the wedding to be at Harenburg Hill…'

'It's a very beautiful church,' Mum said. 'It has a lovely feel inside.'

'Don't tell dear old Donald that,' Wren said, sipping her mineral water. 'He wants to change out the pews to softer chairs…'

'Oh, it's aesthetically beautiful, of course, but that wasn't what I meant,' Mum explained. 'I don't know if it was seeing you and Liam on that stage or whether it was what the previous reverend had said. But there's a good feeling in that place. The Holy Spirit is moving there. And where the Holy Spirit is, there is transformation…'

Chapter 20

'I don't believe we've been formally introduced,' said the old reverend. 'I'm George Williamson, but please, just call me George.'

Wren accepted the hand he offered and shook it. 'Then you must call me Wren.'

'Except on Sundays,' he said with a wink. 'Beautiful wedding, by the way. I couldn't have done it better myself.'

Wren looked over at Ava and Frank as they posed for the photographer, baby bump and all, showered in rose petals outside Harenburg Hill. 'They make a beautiful couple.'

'Speaking of couples,' he said, guiding her by the arm. 'I had no idea Liam Smith was your fiancé when I spoke to him on the phone that day.'

'I'm sorry? What day?'

'He was one of your references,' he said. 'The only one I had to call as a matter of fact.'

'Really?'

'Well, he gave you such a glowing reference, he basically said I would be crazy not to hire you...' George squinted, fixing his attention on Liam in the crowd. 'Any other fiancé might have tried to talk me out it. Not every man wants to move to the country, let alone watch his soon-to-be wife in such a prominent position.'

'As you said before, I'm just a shepherd,' Wren replied.

'True, true... but even shepherds have responsibilities.'

'Of course, but I'm just serving in the way I believe God has called me. Just like Liam,' she gazed at her soon-to-be husband as she spoke. 'His role is no less important, it's just different. He leads worship and facilitates a space where the congregation can focus on the Holy Spirit moving in their midst.'

'Sounds very impressive,' George replied. 'So what do you think it is *you* do?'

'Besides offering an open door,' she began, 'I suppose I decode the Bible as I've been taught and hope to help the congregation understand it better.'

'A Bible hacker.' He nodded. 'I like it. Sounds like you're staying on then?'

Wren paused and peered up at him. 'We've prayed about it…'

'And what do you think the good Lord is telling you to do?'

'Well, we do believe this is where God has called us… at least for now. Until He tells us otherwise, I suppose.'

George beamed and turned to watch the bride and groom revel in yet another passionate embrace. 'Well, Harenburg Hill is all the better for it, I assure you.'

Wren followed his line of sight to see Ava spin around and toss her bouquet of wildflowers into the air. At first, she thought Clare might be a contender, then Zoe. However, a strange autumn breeze blew over the hilltop of Harenburg Hill, carrying the bouquet to land at

Rosemary's feet. Tentatively, Rosemary picked them up to smell them.

'About time that Trevor Burns gets his act together,' George said. 'Maybe this will give him the nudge he needs.'

'I thought I might've seen *you* fighting in there,' Liam said as he approached.

Wren smiled. It had been a long time since she'd seen him in a suit and tie. 'Well, I don't need it,' she told him, raising her left hand and waggling her diamond.

'Well,' George began, 'if you two need a reverend to make that airtight, you know where I am.'

Liam glanced sideways at him. 'How's Saturday?'

'Yeah, I reckon I'm free. I'm meant to meet the boys for golf in the morning – eldership bonding, you see – but I'm sure we can skip a week.'

'Do I have any say in this?' Wren asked.

George shrugged. 'Depends. Are you particularly good at golf, Reverend? They say it's a man's sport…'

Acknowledgements

This story began through breadcrumbs of curiosity before manifesting into a tidal wave that wouldn't release me until the very last word was on the page. For those who have joined me on this whirlwind adventure, thank you...

Daniel – thank you for Margery Jones and for your constant support in every part of this process. This book is not just mine, it's ours, just like everything else in this blessed life. Yours, mine, and God's.

Bella – thank you for your child-like inspiration. You helped me see the township of Brite through a different lens and I am immensely grateful for your unique perspective.

Jeanie and Jenny, my sisters in Christ – thank you for investing your time in me and in this story. Both of us are better for your insight and encouragement.

Finally, thank you to my Heavenly Father, whose mercies are new every day; to my Lord and Saviour Jesus Christ for revealing himself and his grace over my life; and to my constant companion – the Holy Spirit – for guiding my heart and for shaping one woman's mere words into a story. All glory goes to You.

D.O.L.L.

Daughters of Love & Light is a ministry hub for women and an independent publisher of Christian women's literature.

We believe in Christ-centred community, creativity, and calling.

Join the community
www.daughtersofloveandlight.com